SUMMER'S END

D0199988

SUMMER'S END

JOEL A. SUTHERLAND

Scholastic Canada Ltd.
Toronto New York London Auckland Sydney
Mexico City New Delhi Hong Kong Buenos Aires

Scholastic Canada Ltd.
604 King Street West, Toronto, Ontario M5V 1E1, Canada

Scholastic Inc.
557 Broadway, New York, NY 10012, USA

Scholastic Australia Pty Limited
PO Box 579, Gosford, NSW 2250, Australia

Scholastic New Zealand Limited
Private Bag 94407, Botany, Manukau 2163, New Zealand

Scholastic Children's Books
Euston House, 24 Eversholt Street, London NW1 1DB, UK

www.scholastic.ca

Library and Archives Canada Cataloguing in Publication
Sutherland, Joel A., 1980-, author
Summer's end / Joel A. Sutherland.

Issued in print and electronic formats.
ISBN 978-1-4431-3931-1 (paperback).--ISBN 978-1-4431-3932-8 (html)

I. Title.

PS8637.U845S88 2017   jC813'.6   C2016-906225-2
                                                   C2016-906226-0

Cover photos © Shutterstock, Inc: main (Kimberly Palmer), clouds (Jill Battaglia).

6 5 4 3 2 1   Printed in Canada 139   17 18 19 20 21

For Colleen
Forever and always, till the end of time

ONE

June 30

The red cardinal whistled a panicked, pained song. Its wings twitched frantically in the air. The rest of its body lay broken in the dirt, statue still. Its eyes, though. Its eyes — black like tar — were wide open, startled, very much alive. Jacob couldn't peel his own eyes away. The cardinal's gaze was pinned on the four friends — giants towering over the small, dying bird — who ringed it in the woods.

They'd come across the bird as they walked aimlessly through the forest behind Jacob's house, killing time and avoiding grown-ups on the first day of their summer vacation. When they had first set out, their conversation easily shifting from baseball to movies to superheroes, their moods were light and carefree. But now, knowing what they must do to end the bird's suffering, their moods had darkened like a storm cloud.

Hayden picked up a jagged rock the size of a human skull and handed it to Ichiro. "You do it."

"Chicken," Hayden's twin sister, Hannah, said. She punched him lightly on the arm.

"Am not," said Hayden, rubbing his arm gingerly. "And also, ow!"

Hannah tucked her thumbs under her armpits and flapped her arms like wings. "*Bawk, bawk, bawk-bawk-bawk*," she said.

Hayden sighed but didn't say or do anything in response. Since he wasn't putting up a fight, Hannah slowly stopped her chicken imitation, and their focus shifted back to the dying bird and the rock in Ichiro's hand.

Ichiro turned it over and studied its surface, then raised it above his head. For a moment Jacob thought he was actually about to do it. But instead of striking, he lowered the rock slowly.

"No," Ichiro said. "Jake should do it."

"Why?" Jacob asked.

"You're the oldest."

It was true, by two months. A short amount of time that made a world of difference to the three younger friends.

Jacob's birthday was in January, and the twins were born in March of the same year. They were fourteen, but Ichiro's fourteenth birthday was still five months away.

Jacob knew growing up had its advantages. Adults trusted him to be on his own more often. He got to stay up a little later, watch scarier movies. But it also had its drawbacks — more chores, the expectation that he act more mature, being handed a rock.

He took the rock from Ichiro. It was heavier than he expected. It slipped a little in Jacob's fingers, but he managed to get a hold of it before it fell completely from his grasp. He didn't look at his friends, afraid someone might be suppressing a smirk.

A cloud passed overhead and blocked the sun, giving the forest a grey, sluggish aura. A light breeze blew Jacob's hair and chilled the back of his neck. The cool air was welcome and refreshing. The town of Valeton was bracing for a scorcher of a summer. One for the record books. And with the heat would come the storms.

With his free hand Jacob brushed a strand of hair out of his eyes. He looked down on the cardinal. Its wings hadn't stopped twitching.

A string of muscles in Jacob's gut clenched. He tried not to think of the breakfast he'd eaten. He also tried not to think of the bird more than he had to, but that proved to be impossible. He hoped it wasn't a baby, just small. Maybe that would make killing it easier, somehow. Like swatting a mosquito or stepping on an ant. No one hesitates to kill an insect. Why should this be any different? Plus it was a mercy kill, the right thing to do. Leaving the cardinal — baby or not — to die slowly and painfully would be cruel.

So why did it feel so wrong?

A shadow passed between two large trees, about fifteen metres behind Ichiro and the twins. He could have sworn it looked like a boy wearing a red ball cap.

"What are you looking at?" Ichiro asked. He turned around and scanned the woods.

Jacob shrugged. "I don't know. Nothing, I guess," he said weakly, but he couldn't help wondering.

A boy in a red hat. Could it actually have been . . . ? Jacob shook his head. *No, impossible. It's been four years.* And the longer Jacob stared through the woods without seeing anything, the more he began to doubt he'd seen anything at all.

"It was probably just my imagination," he mumbled.

"Jacob," Hannah said, with an edge of urgency but not without kindness, snapping him out of his thoughts. She could switch from sarcasm to sincerity as quickly as a darkened room suddenly lit with golden light. "The bird. It's . . . It's time."

Jacob peeled his sight away from the distant trees and nodded. With a muffled grunt and a clenched jaw, Jacob raised the rock above his head. The forest grew unnaturally quiet, as if the wind and the trees were holding a collective breath. In the sudden silence, the cardinal's panicked whistles were amplified, piercing

Jacob's skull with each rapid trill.

Jacob sighed. He lowered the rock and closed his eyes. "I can't," he whispered.

Without warning someone pulled the rock from his hand. He opened his eyes and saw Hannah, her face as hard as the rock she now held. She cupped it between both hands, high in the air. In a flash she drove it down. It sank a good depth into the soft forest floor, burying the cardinal's crushed body beneath it.

Its left wing — the only part of the bird they could still see — went ramrod straight and then fell limp.

Time passed — a lot or a little, Jacob couldn't say — before he remembered to breathe again. No one spoke. The wind picked up once more, and the leaves rustled their familiar tune. A woodpecker tapped a tree trunk somewhere nearby.

The stone jutted out of the dirt like a tombstone. Jacob pictured himself and his friends dressed in black, someone reciting the Lord's Prayer. With this image in mind he had to suppress a nervous laugh.

Hayden broke the silence. "Hannah, what was that?"

She shrugged. "Someone had to do it. I got tired of waiting."

The three boys couldn't argue with that. Killing the cardinal had to be done, and none of them had been able to do it.

She bent before the rock as if kneeling to pray and yanked it free from the earth.

Ichiro groaned in disgust and Jacob flinched. He quickly looked away. The cardinal's body had been flattened. Blood pooled in tiny pockets of dirt. A small twist of intestine had ruptured through its breast.

Hannah tossed the rock aside. A small red feather was stuck to it. She kicked some dirt over the bird and stared at the forest floor, her expression unreadable.

Jacob had no idea what she was thinking. Nor was he sure he wanted to know.

Hannah's face softened. She even smiled. "C'mon. Let's get out of here and go swimming." She said it as casually as someone who hadn't just crushed a bird with a rock and her own hands. Without waiting for the others to respond, she walked along the path to the country road and the town limit sign where they'd left their bikes.

Jacob's eyes fell back to the thin layer of dirt that failed to fully cover the crushed bird. He groaned and quickly looked away from the gore.

"Well . . ." Ichiro said. After a few silent moments, it became evident whatever else he had planned to say was going to remain unsaid. But Jacob had a good guess what Ichiro and Hayden were thinking. Same thing as him.

It was no surprise that it had fallen to Hannah to kill the cardinal. Jacob had been friends with the twins nearly his entire life. Their house was around the corner from his. They'd been in a few scraps with other kids over the years and Hannah had always held her own. Often, she walked away from fights with fewer bruises and scrapes than anyone, boy or girl. She was tough, both of body and mind.

The grey cloud overhead rolled on, and sunlight once again fell heavily on their shoulders. The air was humid, thick with the earthy smells of an old, cold forest entering a heat wave.

Beads of sweat prickled Hayden's forehead and dripped into his eyes. He wiped his skin and said, "Hannah's got the right idea. Let's go to the beach." The plan sounded good to Jacob too.

They walked quietly, leaving the dead cardinal behind. Their final summer before they split up to go to different high schools lay ahead. The twins were going to Robert Koch Secondary School, while Jacob was going to Valeton's only other public school — Valeton High, which was on the other side of town. Ichiro wasn't only going to a different school — he was moving to a different country. The Miyazakis were leaving for Japan on the third of September, a few days before the start of the school year. Summer break was Jacob's favourite time of year, but this one, he knew, would be bittersweet.

Hannah had already started pedalling away down the road, zigzagging side to side in a carefree manner. Ichiro and Hayden started biking to catch up, leaving Jacob alone for a moment. His bike was leaning against the town sign, which he read for the umpteenth time in his life.

Welcome to
VALETON

Touched by the Past, Embraced by the Future

Population 16,600

Please Keep Our Children Safe

Years ago, someone had spray-painted a line through the word *safe*. Whoever had defaced the sign had done so hastily, and the red paint had run down the sign before it had dried. It was only the previous year that Jacob had finally understood the joke: Please keep our children. Period. And don't bother bringing them back.

Jacob hated that sign, especially the graffiti. It cut too close to the bone.

He mounted his bike and looked back down the path through the trees, into the woods. A cloud of small flies flew through the air and the leaves swayed in the breeze, but Jacob didn't see any other movement. The boy in the red hat wasn't there. As Jacob suspected, he probably never had been there — just a figment of his imagination.

That was for the best. The boy in the red hat and what had happened between them was in the past. It was better not to dwell on it. Not to dwell on *him*.

As for the future, it was better not to dwell on it either — even if he had a bad feeling in his gut whenever he thought about starting grade nine. He didn't know what lay around the corner. By summer's end his life would be different, of that Jacob was sure. So for now he would focus on the present.

He snuck a final wary glance over his shoulder, then pedalled hard to catch up with his friends. "Hey, guys. Wait up."

TWO

July 4

Jacob and Ichiro coasted down the long, curving drive-way. Tall maple and pine trees blotted out the sun and swayed in the wind, creating a soothing symphony of rustling leaves and creaking wood. The boys came to a skidding stop beside Ichiro's house and leaned their bikes against the garage. A little farther downhill sat the lake, gleaming, lapping, calling them toward it.

Nestled on a gently sloping hill on the north bank of Passage Lake, a twenty-five-minute bike ride from the centre of town and a five-minute ride from Twin Pines Resort, Ichiro's house resembled a castle of cement and glass in the woods. Mrs. Miyazaki had a senior management job at the resort, but she had recently accepted a new job in Japan. Ichiro's parents were both from Tokyo and they had long seemed eager for an excuse to return home. Jacob knew Ichiro was dreading moving in September by the way he refused to look at the sold sign on the front lawn every time they passed it.

Jacob left his bike behind and headed for the front door.

"Hey, Jake, hold up," Ichiro said. "We're not going

inside." Without further explanation he turned and walked to a wooded path. Curious, Jacob followed.

The forest floor was covered by a blanket of brown pine needles that crackled underfoot. The twisty path was like a narrow artery choked on both sides by dense green foliage. The air vibrated with the buzz of insects. Jacob swatted a mosquito on his neck, leaving a small smear of blood on his skin, and stepped over a tree root. The path opened into a clearing. In the middle stood a fairly large wooden shed with two doors, sealed by a silver padlock.

"You want to take *Old Kablooey* out on the lake for a paddle?" Jacob asked, guessing why Ichiro had led him to the shed where Mr. Miyazaki's canoe was stored. It was a beat-up blue canoe that had seen better days. Ichiro's father had dubbed it *Old Bluey*. The first time he heard it, Jacob thought Mr. Miyazaki had said *Old Kablooey* and the accidental new name was so fitting that it stuck.

"Yes and no," Ichiro said cryptically. "I have something to show you." He pulled a key out of his pocket, unlocked the doors and swung them open. A little light fell into the shed. They stepped inside. The air was thick and musty. Slowly, Jacob's eyes adjusted to the darkness.

Every shelf, every corner, every nook and cranny was

packed with *stuff*. Gardening stuff, home repair stuff and, best of all, fun stuff: lawn darts and horseshoes and croquet mallets, inflatable rafts and beach balls and water guns. And in the middle of the floor was *Old Kablooey*. Jacob thought that was odd because they had suspended it from the ceiling rafters the last time they had gone canoeing, just a few days before.

And then he saw something that made him forget everything else. It was hanging in *Old Kablooey*'s spot. A gorgeous, brand-new red canoe. Jacob walked over to it and ran his hand along the starboard gunwale. The craft was sleek, expertly made and could seat four with room to spare.

"Happy Independence Day!" Ichiro said, spreading his arms and grinning widely.

"We're not American," Jacob pointed out dryly.

"True, but let's not let that stop us from celebrating. My dad bought it yesterday."

"But you're moving in, like, two months."

"Yeah," Ichiro said. "He knows I'm not happy about it. I guess he feels bad. Mom was pretty angry when he brought it home, but we can probably sell it for some decent cash before we move, so she agreed to let me keep it."

Jacob allowed his eyes to continue feasting on the red canoe and whistled. "This is so much nicer than *Old*

Kablooey." He looked at the sad, battered blue canoe as if it were a pitiful living thing and added, "No offence."

Ichiro laughed. "I haven't put it in the water yet. I thought I'd wait for you."

Jacob answered by flipping a bucket upside down and stepping on it to unlatch one of the cords that strung the canoe to the roof. Ichiro took care of the other side. The canoe was surprisingly light. They lowered it to the ground and tossed a couple of paddles and life jackets in its hull.

The boys carried it by the handholds down the hill to the edge of the lake and slid it into the water. The red paint cast a crimson reflection like a bloodstain around the canoe. They put on their life jackets, climbed in and sat in silence for a moment, relishing the gentle rocking of the boat and the sound of waves lapping against its sides.

"Where to?" Ichiro asked.

"Anywhere," Jacob said. That was the beauty of it. Thanks to its horrible condition, they had been too afraid to take *Old Kablooey* far from Ichiro's house. This new canoe equalled freedom. They could go anywhere. It was the beginning of summer vacation, they had no responsibilities and it didn't matter where they went or what they did. Fun was guaranteed.

"Aye, aye," Ichiro said. "*Scarlet Sails* is setting out for adventure. Destination: unknown."

"You named the canoe *Scarlet Sails*?"

"I did."

"Even though canoes don't have sails?"

"I never said it was a good name."

"What are you, three years old?"

"Hey, man, I'm not the only one who gives stuff lame names. I know you called your teddy bear Mr. Jingles."

"Yeah," Jacob said, "when I was *three*."

"But you still sleep with Mr. Jingles, don't you?"

Jacob chose to ignore that comment and directed the conversation back to *Scarlet Sails*. "Well, it could've been worse. You could've named the canoe *Emerald Engine*. Or *Purple Propeller*."

"Don't be dumb. I might not be a boat expert, but I know colours."

Jacob laughed and dipped his paddle into the water with a satisfying splash. They pushed off the shore and cut into Passage Lake. Their strokes fell into a rhythm and they picked up speed quickly. The golden sun beat warmly on their backs as they passed million-dollar summer homes. Some were owned by movie stars and pro athletes who vacationed in Muskoka, but most were owned by wealthy business people. A speedboat rumbled past, pulling a water skier who waved at the boys. They waved back.

Time dipped and dived with their paddles, leading around bends, past bays, through creeks, taking them deeper into Passage Lake and farther from home. A multitude of small rocky islands dotted the water, some home to cottages, some too small to fit more than a tent.

Ichiro pulled his paddle out of the water and Jacob followed his lead. They hadn't taken a break for a long time and his muscles burned. It was a good feeling.

"Would you rather fight one hundred duck-sized horses," Ichiro asked, "or one horse-sized duck?"

"What?" Jacob shook his head and wondered if he'd heard his friend correctly.

"It's a very simple question," Ichiro said with mock restraint. "One hundred duck-sized horses or one horse-sized duck. Who would you rather fight? You know, to the death?"

So Jacob *had* heard Ichiro correctly. He shrugged his shoulders, gave the question a little thought, and then dived right in. "Do I have any magical or super powers?"

"Why would you think that?"

"I'm fighting ducks or horses that have swapped sizes. I'm assuming this battle isn't taking place in the world as we know it."

Ichiro considered Jacob's question. "No powers. It's hand-to-hand combat. Or, well, hand-to-hoof-or-webbed-foot combat."

"Do I have to fight the one hundred horses at the same time, or one after the other?"

"Why would they line up and wait their turn? The horses might be miniature, but they're not idiots. They're coming at you all at once."

"All right," Jacob said with a nod. "I'll fight the horses. What are they going to do, run over my toes until I give in? A giant duck, on the other hand, has a giant beak. One hundred duck-sized horses — that's the correct answer."

"There's no right or wrong answer," Ichiro said. "But yeah, the horses are totally correct. Only a crazy person would pick the horse-sized duck. What about this? If you could be any of the X-Men, who would you be?"

Jacob considered the new question for a moment, but Ichiro answered first, as if he'd asked it more to make a statement than to hear Jacob's answer.

"I'd be Wolverine so I could heal myself. And so I could make claws jut out of my hands." He made a fist and ran a finger over his knuckles. "What about you?"

"Healing and claws would be cool," Jacob said, nodding and staring at the shore across the water. "But I'd be Professor X."

"Professor X? Why? Mind reading?"

"No. Not for his powers. Because he starts a school to protect other mutants and makes new friends, like a family."

"You have friends. And family," Ichiro said. "Your mother."

"I love my mom, but it's just the two of us and she works a lot."

Ichiro nodded sympathetically. "Well, we can hang out all summer long."

"Thanks, man. I appreciate that. I just want to play baseball, ride our bikes around town and canoe."

"That sounds awesome." Ichiro smiled with a faraway look in his eyes. "I want to make the most of this summer too, you know? I'm not exactly jumping for joy at the thought of moving. Just because my parents are from Japan doesn't mean it's going to be easy for me. I've never been there. Everything looks completely different from Canada, and I mean everything. I don't even speak much Japanese. What if I ask for some chocolate ice cream in a restaurant and accidentally order octopus ice cream?"

"Octopus ice cream? You made that up."

"Did not! I saw it on YouTube! This guy did a video review and ate, like, half a tub of the stuff. I'm not even kidding." Ichiro pretended to vomit and they laughed together.

"Look, I get it," Jacob said. "You're worried next year is going to suck. I'm worried too. So let's make sure this is an epic summer. One we'll never forget. Deal?"

"Yeah, man. Deal." Ichiro turned his gaze and scanned the shores of the lake. There was a marsh, nearly hidden by the overgrowth of large trees and wild bushes, not too far from where they sat. "How about we check out what's down that way and then head home?"

"Sure," Jacob said. "No time like the present to start our epic summer."

They began to paddle again and the canoe slowly picked up a little speed. Their wake was an ever-widening V, tiny ripples of water that rolled to shore. Small cottages — the type that have curtains for bedroom walls, creaky floorboards and sinks with hand pumps — surrounded this part of the lake, packed tightly together. But they petered out the closer the boys got to the marsh. There must have been more than fifty metres between the last cottage and the waterway's opening, which was odd. There was plenty of room for another two or three small summer dwellings there.

Somewhere across the lake an owl hooted, and the sound carried clean across the water as if the bird was right beside them.

Hoot. Hoot. Hoot.

Hoo—

The bird's call died abruptly as Jacob steered the canoe into the marsh, and there were no other sounds of life. Craggy trees and plants grew wild in tangled walls on both sides of the marsh, so thick and twisted that very little sunlight passed through. Everything was dark green, brown and black. The canoe's colour was so bright in comparison to the overgrowth that it seemed unnaturally red.

They passed a row of rotten wooden posts that jutted out of the murky water. It looked to Jacob like the submerged skeleton of a drowned sea monster left to decompose in this watery wasteland where time seemed to slow to a crawl.

"Make me a promise, Jake," Ichiro said. His voice echoed back.

"Sure, what?"

"If I get eaten by the Kalapik, tell my parents I love them. Then delete my computer's browsing history."

Jacob laughed. "There's no such thing as the Kalapik."

"Yeah, I know. But if he did exist, this is where he'd live."

In his mind, Jacob was suddenly a six-year-old boy again, being tucked in at night by his mother. She reached for the switch on his bedside lamp and hesitated. "You know what you did today was wrong, right, Jake?"

Young Jacob pulled his bedsheet up to his chin and nodded.

"I was so scared. I thought I'd lost you." Tears welled in her eyes. She nearly stopped talking, and then continued. "I thought the Kalapik had gotten you."

A shiver spread through Jacob's body. "What's the Kalapik?"

His mother sighed. "A monster with green skin, black eyes, long hair and claws for fingernails. It lives at the bottom of the lake and steals children who disobey their parents, and then keeps them forever. You must never, ever go swimming alone again. Do you hear me?"

He burst out crying and clenched his mother's arm and promised never to go in the lake without her again. He pleaded with her to leave the light on and stay all night in his room, in his bed, right beside him, so the Kalapik wouldn't take him away.

He soon discovered that other parents had also warned kids at his school not to go swimming or boating alone lest the Kalapik drag them down to the bottom of the lake. And a few years later, when Jacob was ten, a classmate named Colton disappeared. A search party combed the woods, and the police dragged the bottom of every lake within a thirty kilometre radius of Valeton, but the boy's body was never discovered. Although most kids in Jacob's class were too old to believe that there was a monster at the bottom of one of Valeton's lakes, it didn't take long for a rumour to spread through the school that Colton's paddleboat was found adrift somewhere in the lake and he was the Kalapik's latest victim.

That was ridiculous, of course. As Jacob grew older he realized that the town's adults used the legend of the Kalapik as a scare tactic, a way of keeping their young children out of the water unsupervised. A young kid swimming in the lake alone could drown. A young kid too scared of a monster to dip a single toe in the water could not.

"Don't you think, Jake?" Ichiro asked, a hint of annoyance creeping into his tone.

The sound of his friend's voice ripped Jacob out of the past and back to the present, back to the red canoe, back to the dark marsh. "Don't I think what?"

"That this looks like it could be where the Kalapik lives?"

"Oh, um," Jacob said, as he straightened his back and cleared his throat. "Yeah, I guess it does." He didn't want to talk about the Kalapik any longer. He'd managed to keep the creature, and Colton, out of his thoughts for a few years, and he'd rather keep it that way. Luckily, he spotted something that allowed him to change the subject.

"Look up ahead," Jacob said.

The marsh opened up into a larger body of water, allowing sunlight to pass through once again. They paddled into the open water and took in their new surroundings. The water was clean and calm, ideal for swimming, and the trees were tall and lush. There was even a rocky cliff, ten metres tall, on the far shore, both scenic and perfect for cliff jumping. And yet there wasn't a single cottage or home anywhere to be seen. It was as if they'd paddled into a separate lake forgotten by time, an undiscovered body of water. *Like early explorers*, Jacob thought.

"Toto, I've a feeling we're not in Kansas anymore," Ichiro said. "This must be a different lake, right? This is even nicer than Passage Lake."

Jacob searched his memory, recalling a map of the area he'd studied before. "Yeah, I think it's called . . . Seppu . . . Seppuk . . . oh, I remember. Sepequoi Lake."

The lake and surrounding woods were silent, and the splash of their paddles sounded muffled. Jacob rubbed his ears. They felt like they were under tremendous pressure.

Ichiro rubbed his ears too. "You feel that?" he asked.

"Yes. What's causing it?"

"Dunno."

As they rubbed their ears and talked about the odd sensation, it slowly dissipated. The water gently lapping against the side of the canoe suddenly sounded louder than usual. It seemed to play a quiet and sooth-ing melody. *Splish-splish splash. Splish-splish splash. Splish-splish splash splash, splash-splash-splash.*

Sitting in the dead centre of the water was a single solitary island. It was choked with dark trees that con-cealed what lay at its centre. Grey rock with streaks of red minerals ringed the island's shore.

They began to paddle again and travelled the rest of the distance to the island in silence. It didn't look too far away, but perhaps by optical illusion, the island appeared to retreat as they neared it. Ash-grey clouds stretched across the sky like a veil.

Then, as if time had skipped a beat, the island sud-denly loomed before them, its tall pines towering over-head. Without wind to bend their branches, the trees stood still as statues.

The canoe bumped gently against the rock and slow-ly twisted to sit parallel with the shore.

"I have a strange feeling about this place," Jacob said, trying to look through the trees but seeing only darkness.

"Me too," Ichiro said.

"Do you want to head back home?"

"Are you kidding me?" Ichiro smiled. "This island is weird and, yeah, I'll admit it, a little creepy. There's no way I'm going home before we check it out!"

Jacob returned the smile. "Good. Me too."

He picked up the rope and looked for a low-hanging branch sturdy enough to secure the canoe.

"Wait," Ichiro said. He pointed over Jacob's shoulder.

There, not too far away, was a dock. It was old and beaten but solid enough to hold their craft in calm waters.

How did we not see that before? Jacob asked himself. They paddled over and Jacob hopped out. He tied the rope to a cleat and helped Ichiro onto the dock. The wood shifted and groaned beneath their weight. The boys walked to land before the dock decided it didn't want to hold them any longer.

A thin path cut a dark hole through the woods. It looked like it had once been wide enough for a truck to pass through, but the bush had reclaimed it over time. Now it appeared to be used only by passing wildlife.

Jacob felt something pulling him forward, daring him to look.

For such a quiet, isolated island, there was a ton of energy in the air. It made it hard to focus, difficult to think. The small tendrils of an oncoming headache worked their way into the extremities of Jacob's brain. He closed his eyes and rubbed his forehead.

"Hey, look." Ichiro, oblivious to Jacob's discomfort, pointed above their heads. A piece of rusted metal peeked out from behind a few branches. It was curved and shaped into an intricate lacework. A single word could be seen through the leaves:

END

Jacob grabbed a branch and bent it so they could read the rest of the sign. The branch snapped immediately and he dropped it to the ground. It looked healthy on the outside but the centre of the branch was black and decaying. It looked like a broken bone with rotten marrow at its core. The tree was dying slowly from the inside out. *Heart rot*, Jacob knew. A fungal disease. But he thought it only affected old trees, not trees so small and young.

He could now read the rest of the sign:

SUMMER'S END

"It's a gate," Ichiro said.

"On an island. In the middle of nowhere. What is this place?"

"No idea."

Jacob shrugged. "Let's find out."

The air was hotter and heavier the farther inland they walked. It wasn't altogether unpleasant, and smelled of moss and summer berries. Jacob saw plenty of moss — it coated the floor like a spongy green carpet — but there were no berries.

"You know what's weird?" Ichiro asked, as they ducked under branches and twisted their bodies through the overgrowth.

Plenty, Jacob thought. *Plenty's weird about this island.* "What?"

"I haven't been bitten by a single mosquito. Haven't even had to swat one away."

Bush this dense, that was weird.

They carried on toward the centre of the island in silence.

Another few steps and the path suddenly ended, widening to reveal a large clearing. A crushed stone walkway led to the front door of a large house.

Jacob's headache began to fade.

The house sat at the far side of the clearing, surrounded by trees and tangled bushes. Against the backdrop of the grey sky, its red-brick chimney looked out of place — the only splash of colour on the black and grey house. The lack of colour made the house look like a dead thing, a pile of bones stripped clean of flesh by time and sun and rain. The sloped roof and a large bay window above the front door gave the old building a hunched look. A dormer window jutted out of the second floor. When Jacob looked away he thought he saw a flash of movement in the window out of the corner of his eye, but when he looked again there was nothing there. The house's face was scarred by cracks in its rotting wooden boards, and most of the first-floor windows were dirty and shuttered. The porch was caked in mud, but the front door appeared to be in surprisingly good shape.

On a rusty pole beside the house, in a flower bed overgrown by weeds, was a wrought-iron sign that was a twin to the one they'd seen near the dock:

SUMMER'S END

"So this is Summer's End," Ichiro said. "What do you think has better odds: That a serial killer lives here or a crazy old cat lady?"

"For our sake, I hope neither," Jacob responded. "Have you ever seen a place like this?"

Ichiro shook his head.

"It looks like it hasn't been lived in for decades."

"No kidding," Ichiro said. "The serial killer cat lady should spend a little time fixing the joint up."

Jacob's laughter was genuine but contained a shred of nervousness. "Let me guess: you want to look inside."

"I want to look inside," Ichiro said.

"So do I." He looked at his watch. It was a couple of minutes past six o'clock. His mother had picked up an extra shift at The Hot Plate and wouldn't be home until late, but Jacob didn't want to still be on the lake when it started getting dark. "Five minutes. Then we should head back."

"Sure." As they crossed the clearing, Ichiro pointed to a crumbling stone well covered in moss and vines. "That's where I'd dump the body parts. You know, if I was a serial killer — with twenty-nine cats."

The front steps sagged as they walked on them. After a brief moment of hesitation, he found the courage to knock on the front door. The sound echoed across the clearing. They listened for the sound of footsteps on the other side of the door, but heard nothing but the wind behind their backs. Jacob gripped the door handle but pulled his hand back immediately.

"What is it?" Ichiro asked.

"It's cold." He tentatively grabbed the handle once more. The thick door was fastened to its frame with large iron hinges. It was so heavy that Jacob had to push it open with his shoulder, but it swung open without a sound.

Shafts of light streamed into the front entrance through the open door.

"He-hello?" Jacob called out. He hoped Ichiro wouldn't give him a hard time later about his voice cracking. "Is anyone here?"

No one answered.

Dust painted every surface. Tangled strands of cobweb clung to the ceiling. A long, narrow hallway was dissected by four closed doors, concealing whatever lay in wait behind them.

Jacob began to picture an assortment of horrors hiding behind each of the doors. He'd watched too many horror movies, read too many Stephen King books, and his imagination was making things worse than they were. This was just an old house that hadn't been lived in for years. Nothing else.

"All right," he said, "I've seen enough for now. We can go."

Ichiro nodded distractedly. His gaze had fallen on a small table near the front door. A snow globe with a boy and a girl building a snowman caught his attention and he picked it up. It played a few chiming notes in his hand, a holdover from the time someone had turned the metal crank long ago. The unexpected music startled Ichiro and he nearly dropped the globe. Jacob flinched and looked around wildly, fearful that the music might awaken something. His imagination, once again getting the better of him. What had he expected to happen? Some madman to burst through one of the doors with an axe?

Nothing happened. Ichiro placed the globe back down on its circular footprint in the dust.

Beside it was a wooden photo frame with words carved into it:

Family
Where life begins
and love never ends . . .

There was a torn piece of glossy paper in the bottom of the frame, as if an old photograph had been quickly removed. Ichiro picked up the frame for a closer look.

Something shiny caught Jacob's eye. "What's that? On the back?"

Ichiro turned the frame over. It was a necklace, taped to the back of the frame. Ichiro peeled the necklace free. The yellowed tape practically disintegrated at his touch. The necklace was silver. Dangling from the thin chain was a pendant in the shape of a capital C. At the tip of the C was a small red gemstone that resembled the mineral that was embedded in the rocky shoreline of the island.

It twirled hypnotically as Jacob wondered who it might have belonged to and why they had hidden it in the front hall.

Before he had time to figure it out, a shadow passed over the wall at the end of the hall. The pitter-patter of small, bare feet echoed through the house. A medicinal smell seeped into the air.

"What was that?" Jacob whispered urgently. His body seized up.

"I don't know," Ichiro said. "Let's get out of here." The necklace slipped from his fingers, clattered to the floor and slid under the table, but the sound fell on deaf ears.

The boys turned and ran out of the house. Without pausing to shut the front door, they sprinted past the sign, past the well and across the clearing. At the edge of the woods they stopped and looked back.

Time stood still. A cool wind swept through the trees, bending the grass and making the ground look like a rolling wave. The surrounding trees rustled impatiently. Jacob took his first breath since they'd fled. He stared at the open door with wide eyes.

Something moved inside. He grabbed Ichiro's arm and prepared to run again, but then the something hopped out of the door, down the front steps and landed gently in the grass.

It was a rabbit. It stood up on its back legs and looked in their direction, its nose twitching and its straight ears swivelling side to side. After a moment it hopped away into the woods.

Jacob and Ichiro burst out laughing, and their bodies shook for the better part of a minute. Jacob punched Ichiro playfully on the arm and Ichiro hit him back. They turned and headed back to the canoe.

"I knew it was a bunny all along," Ichiro said.

"Liar! I saw your face. You were as scared as I was."

"Okay, fine. The bunny freaked me out." Ichiro brushed a low-hanging branch of pine needles out of the way as they walked.

As they neared the water, away from the heart of the island, away from the house, Jacob's feet felt heavier. Like his shoes were full of water. As if something was trying to keep him there.

The world was a silhouette, the trees nothing but black shadows and outlines against the blazing summer sky. The canoe banged gently against the side of the dock.

As they paddled out into the sparkling golden lake, Jacob said, "This island is pretty cool."

Ichiro turned around to face Jacob. "Yeah. I'm going to my aunt's tomorrow, but let's come back soon. This could be our summer hangout. I think there's a lot more to see. What do you think?"

"I don't think I could stay away if I wanted to," Jacob said.

For some reason he couldn't quite explain, he

instantly felt a twinge of doubt and anxiety. He shook it off and dipped his paddle into the calm water.

Before them, the sun lit their route home. Behind, whorls of mist drifted off the lake's surface and encircled the island, wrapping it in fog.

THREE

July 5

Jacob ran as fast as he could, but it wasn't fast enough. He leapt over roots and rocks and ducked under low-hanging branches. His heart pounded against his chest. His lungs burned and wheezed. He pumped his legs harder, swung his arms quicker, and yet he was too slow.

He was going to die.

The creature closed in on him.

Miraculously, Jacob reached the edge of the woods before he was caught, but then—

He came to a skidding stop and ground his feet into the dirt. He had nearly run straight off the edge of a cliff. He peered wildly over the ledge. The drop appeared to be more than five hundred metres. It felt like he was balancing atop the tip of the CN Tower. Below — far, far below — was a cool blue sheet of water, solid as concrete and calling his name.

Jacob spun around, but it was too late.

The bunny burst through the treeline and flew through the air with a mad shriek. Jacob raised his arms to block his face and caught the bunny in his hands. He tumbled backwards and they both fell down, down, down . . .

Jacob woke up before he hit the water. It took him a moment to realize he'd been dreaming. In his hands he clutched Mr. Jingles. He tossed the teddy bear aside and stared at his ceiling as he waited for a lingering feeling of vertigo to pass. Slowly, his heart rate returned to normal.

"Stupid bunny," he mumbled.

He grabbed his phone off the bedside table and checked the time: 10:07. He texted Ichiro,

whats up

then played a few games of Angry Birds, but he couldn't focus enough to do much damage to the green piggies. He casually tossed his phone on the bed beside him, then rubbed some sleep out of his eyes.

His phone dinged. Ichiro had texted back.

the sky

lame

I want to go back
to the island. you?

A moment later, his phone chimed again.

Definitely.
Dreamt about it all night.
Let's go when I get back
from my aunt's house. k?

k

He opened a browser and searched "Sepequoi Lake." He was right about the name. He tapped a map and zoomed in. He could see the short waterway that connected it to Passage Lake. There in the centre of the small lake was the island they had discovered. He zoomed in as far as the map would allow, hoping a name would appear, but none did. He switched to satellite view and the island turned brown and green, but Summer's End wasn't visible — the house must have been obscured by the island's tall trees. Jacob's stomach growled. He turned off his phone and went downstairs in search of food.

The kitchen was filled with the rich aromas of bacon, eggs, cheese and fresh-ground coffee beans. His mother was sitting at the table, sipping from a steaming mug and working on a newspaper crossword puzzle.

"Sleepyhead," she said, without looking up when he entered. A mid-morning sunbeam cut a path across the centre of the kitchen table.

"It's, like, ten after ten," Jacob said. "Most of my friends don't get up before noon."

"Huh?" She looked up from the table and frowned at her son, then a look of understanding softened her face and she laughed. "Oh, no, not you. A ten-letter word for a tired person. Sleepyhead. It's twenty-seven across." She tapped her finger on the crossword puzzle.

"Ah, I see," Jacob said, raising his hands and smiling. "All is forgiven."

"Well, thank God for that." His mother returned the smile and turned back to her crossword. "There's breakfast casserole in the oven. Help yourself."

"Thanks, Mom." Jacob wasted no time grabbing a plate and scooping a piece of casserole. Steam escaped from between the layers of bread, and gooey processed cheese melted out onto the plate. It was his favourite breakfast. He poured a glass of orange juice, took a sip and began to feel a little more human. His weird bunny dream had faded away to oblivion.

After he'd polished off his first helping of casserole and returned to the table with his second, his mother put her pencil down.

"So, are you going to tell me why you were late getting home last night?"

"Uh . . ." Jacob stalled, then decided there was no need to lie. He hadn't done anything wrong. "You had to work late so I didn't think you'd mind. How'd you know?"

"I called your cell but you didn't answer, so I called home and you didn't pick up."

"Why?"

"I couldn't find my necklace and thought it might've fallen off outside. I was hoping you could check for me. And don't change the subject."

"Did you find it? Your necklace?"

She pulled the necklace out from under her shirt collar. It was a silver chain with a green gemstone pendant. "It was in the dish on my nightstand when I got home. I guess I forgot to put it on. And once again, don't change the subject."

Jacob raised his hands in mock surrender and laughed. "All right, all right. I can't get anything past you, can I?"

"Of course not. I'm your mother."

"Well, here's the truth," he said, deciding to only share *half* the truth. "Ichiro got this awesome new canoe — he gave it a dumb name, but it's still awesome — and we took it out on the lake. It was pretty awesome, and time just kinda slipped away. But I knew you picked up an extra shift so I thought it was no big deal. Did I mention how awesome it was?"

"Yeah, I think you covered that. But why didn't you answer your phone?"

"It didn't ring." Jacob took his phone out of his pocket and checked his call history, then showed the screen to this mother. "There's no record you called."

"That's weird." She looked at her own phone's call history. "Right here, it shows I called you at 6:06."

"We were—" Jacob stopped speaking. He'd been about to say "on the island," but decided to rewrite

38

history, only slightly. "We were paddling home at that time. Technology, eh?"

"Yeah, I guess. Well, I'm glad you weren't ignoring me. This is silly, but when you didn't answer I thought of the Kalapik for the first time in years."

"I'm not a little kid anymore, Mom. You don't need to worry about me."

"I'll worry about you for as long as I'd like, which will be forever, FYI. It's what we moms do."

"It's funny," Jacob said, although it wasn't actually funny at all, "Ichiro talked about the Kalapik yesterday too." He shovelled another fork of casserole into his mouth, fearful he might soon lose his appetite thanks to the direction the conversation was headed, and not wanting to waste a bite. "It seems a little twisted to lie like that to kids, don't you think?"

His mother sighed. "I used the Kalapik as a way to keep you safe when you were too young to go into the lake on your own. All the parents in town did the same, including mine when I was young. You'll understand when you have kids of your own, Jake. You'll do anything and say anything to keep them safe."

"Even lie?"

"Yes, even lie. And the Kalapik is only a white lie. So many kids have disappeared without a trace over the years."

"Like Colton," Jacob said flatly.

"Yes, like Colton. I remember thinking, if it could happen to him, it could happen to you. To this day I see his mother wandering around town, muttering nonsense to herself. She was never the same after her son vanished. After her husband . . ."

Jacob's mother trailed off, as if she didn't want to tell her son what had happened to Colton's family after he disappeared, but Jacob knew. Valeton was a small town, so everyone knew. Colton's father had hanged himself in the attic, and his mother — already mired in a deep depression — snapped. She spent her days walking up and down Main Street in her dirty purple housecoat, talking to herself and pleading with passersby. *"Help me, help me,"* Jacob had heard her say the previous fall as he rode past on his bike. *"Help my boy."* He had slowed down temporarily but pedalled away fast when she locked eyes with him. A cold shiver had spread up and down his spine.

"Anyway," Jacob's mother said, pulling Jacob back to the present day and their kitchen table, "I didn't want to end up like Colton's mom, or any of the other parents who have lost their children to Passage Lake. That's why I scared you with stories of the Kalapik. He's just Valeton's own personal bogeyman, invented years ago out of a desire to keep our children safe." She exhaled sharply through her nose, a half laugh. "And let me tell you, he works."

No kidding, Jacob thought. But how safe *were* Valeton's children? He thought of the town limit sign. *Please keep our children.*

And don't bother bringing them back.

He pushed the thought out of his mind and said, "I get it, Mom."

"I love you, Jake. With all my heart. So next time you're going to stay out with your friends, just send me a text, okay?"

"Of course, no problem." He stood, gave her a hug and took his plate to the sink. "Well, as long as my cellphone works next time Ichiro and I go out canoeing."

His mother nodded. "Stay away from whatever dead zone you two paddled into yesterday."

Jacob left the kitchen without answering. There was no way he was going to agree to that request. If he had his way he'd already be in the canoe on his way back to Sepequoi Lake, back to the island, back to Summer's End.

FOUR

July 11

The sky was such a bright, bold blue that it was difficult to recall how creepy Summer's End had looked the first time they found it, a week before.

"Not that I want my parents to feel like they have to buy my love," Ichiro said, "but I am really happy they bought me *Scarlet Sails* in order to buy my love."

"Me too. But I gotta say, that's still a stupid name." They laughed, and Jacob grabbed the door handle. It was still cold even though it had the full intensity of the summer sun on it.

"Wait," Ichiro said tensely.

Jacob flinched. "What?"

"Before you open the door, don't forget: beware of bunnies."

"You better beware my fists if you freak me out like that again," Jacob said in good humour. He opened the door, then frowned. "Hey, Ichiro?"

"Yes?" Ichiro said warily.

"Didn't we leave the door open when we ran away?"

"The wind probably blew it closed," Ichiro said, but his tone didn't sound very confident.

They both peered inside for a moment before going in.

In the front foyer, Ichiro looked back at the open door. "Don't bother closing it."

"I wasn't going to."

Although it was a beautiful July day outside and warm sunlight poured in through the doorway, the windows and some holes in the exterior walls, the hallway was cold and dark. Everything remained exactly as it had been before. The hall table, the frame with the carved quote, the snow globe, the spiderwebs and the dust.

"No bunny," Jacob said.

"No bunny," Ichiro confirmed.

It was meant to be a joke, but neither boy laughed.

"I didn't notice this before, but the wood here looks darker than farther down the hallway." Ichiro pointed at the floor and moved his hand in a wide circle around their feet.

Jacob crouched and scraped the wood with his thumbnail. Something dark brown came off and remained beneath his nail. "It's stained or something."

Ichiro cleared his throat. "Wanna keep going?"

"We came all this way," Jacob said with a shrug, rubbing his hand on his shorts and wishing he hadn't touched the dirty floor. He wasn't so sure he did want to go any farther. But he couldn't say that aloud. Ichiro might never let him live it down, despite the fact that Ichiro wasn't exactly racing ahead either.

They looked at each of the closed doors, up and down the hall, like nervous contestants on a game show. *I'll take what's behind door number three!*

"Well, where to first?" Ichiro asked.

"Why don't we start on the left and make our way clockwise around the main floor?"

"Good idea. That's why you're the leader."

"Who said I was the leader?"

"I did, just now." Ichiro waved to the first door on their left. "Partly because you're so smart, and partly because that means you have to go first."

Jacob sighed but led the way through the doorway into what appeared to be a parlour. Heavy curtains covered the windows, draping the room in darkness. Their eyes gradually adjusted to the change in light, slowly revealing the room's secrets. A floral-print couch and chair with wooden legs were pushed up against the wall and faced an antique record player — the type with a large horn and a hand crank on the side — that sat on a small table under a blanket of dust. A small metal plaque on the base of the record player read, *Victor V Phonograph*. Paintings of lakes and forests hung on the walls, as well as a framed piece of cross-stitch that read *Family is everything.* Other than the dust and the dirt and the tangled strands of old cobwebs hanging from ceiling corners and lampshades, it looked like the room was still lived in. Like someone might enter behind them at any moment, take a seat on the couch and start listening to some music.

Jacob crossed the room to get a better look at the phonograph. He'd never seen one in real life before, only in pictures and movies.

"This is pretty cool," he said. There was a record under the needle. He wiped a layer of dust off its face, revealing the label.

Wiegenlied, op. 49, no. 4
Guten Abend, gute Nacht
Johannes Brahms

"It's German," Jacob said, as Ichiro approached and peered over his shoulder at the record.

"I didn't know you spoke German," Ichiro said.

"I don't, but I recognize it. I think *guten* means 'good' and *nacht* means 'night.'"

"Well, good night to you too, Mr. Brahms. C'mon," he said, with a smile and a nudge. "There's nothing useful here. Let's keep moving."

Jacob took one last look at the phonograph. He would've loved to see if it still worked, but Ichiro had already disappeared from his sight and he wasn't completely comfortable with the thought of being alone in the house.

It's so old, it probably doesn't work, he told himself in an attempt to feel a little better about moving on without testing the hand crank.

He started to follow Ichiro into the next room. The wooden floorboards creaked as he passed over them. For a disorienting moment, it sounded like a set of footsteps trailed him. He stopped and looked over his shoulder, back into the parlour. Couch, chair, table, phonograph . . . Everything appeared the same as before.

Once he was satisfied that he must have imagined the sound of footsteps, he caught up to Ichiro in the next room. It wasn't much larger than the ornate dining table that dominated it. The table was bigger than any Jacob had ever seen. A dozen chairs surrounded it, and candles burned down to their metal holders sat in the centre of the table. A hutch with glass doors, filled with fine china plates, bowls and crystal glasses, sat against the wall.

"I'm so hungry," Ichiro said, looking longingly at the hutch. "Why didn't we think to bring some snacks?" He slid open a drawer and gazed inside. It was filled with silverware. "Hey, Jake. Look at this."

He pulled out an old photograph that had been

hidden under the cutlery. The paper was wrinkled and the image was sepia toned. It was a picture of a man and woman on their wedding day, dressed in old-fashioned clothing. The stern-looking, bearded groom sat on a wooden chair while the skinny, dark-haired bride stood behind him holding a bouquet of flowers. The whites of her eyes seemed unnaturally bright, as if the photograph had been overexposed in places.

"The corner's ripped," Ichiro said.

Jacob thought of the empty photo frame in the front hall. It had a small piece of torn paper in it. He reminded Ichiro of the frame. "The picture must've been ripped out and hidden in the drawer. Maybe the couple had a fight?"

"You're a genius."

Jacob shook his head. "Not really. I'm just good at connecting dots. Turn it over," he said, pointing at the old photograph.

Ichiro did so, revealing cursive handwriting on the back:

James and Tresa, 1906
A grand adventure is about to begin.

"Tresa?" Ichiro said. "I've never heard that name before." He turned the photograph back over and stared into her piercing eyes. "She sure was pretty."

The fine hair on Jacob's forearms stood on end. He scanned the room quickly. Ichiro was still the only other person there, but he had briefly felt like he was being watched. He stole one more glance behind him and then looked back at the photo.

"They must have lived here a long time ago," Jacob said. He wondered if anyone had lived in the house since the early 1900s. If anyone had, they hadn't done any redecorating. Thanks to the antique furniture, the phonograph and the ancient photograph, it was easy to picture James and Tresa still living there today.

"Hey," Jacob said, as a thought dawned on him. "Shouldn't this place be, like, empty?" He remembered a house in his neighbourhood that had been boarded up a couple of years back. He and Ichiro had snuck in and wandered around. There wasn't a single piece of furniture in any of the rooms, and the walls were covered in spray paint, obscene messages and crude drawings no doubt left behind by teenagers. "Why did the last people who lived here leave all their stuff behind?"

"Maybe someone still owns the house. Maybe it's just rundown, not abandoned."

Jacob raised his eyebrows and nodded, impressed. "You're probably right. Look at the big brains on you!"

Ichiro placed the photograph back in the hutch and

took a bow. "Thank you, thank you."

They carried on to the next room, at the back of the house, which turned out to be the kitchen. Jacob opened an old-fashioned wooden refrigerator (a gold plate on the front door read *McCray 1905*) and a gust of hot, mouldering air assaulted their noses.

"Close it, close it!" Ichiro shouted. He took a step back and waved his hand in front of his face.

Even after the door was closed, the odour languished in the room. Jacob crossed the kitchen and knocked over a chair in his haste. It clattered to the tile floor. The sound echoed hollowly throughout the kitchen. Jacob bent to pick up the chair. Out of the corner of his eye he saw a shadow pass through the kitchen.

"Did you see that?" he asked. It had happened so quickly, he couldn't be sure of what he'd seen.

"See what?" Ichiro asked.

"Nothing," Jacob said. He shook his head and rubbed his face. "I guess this place is making me jumpy."

There was another phrase on the wall near the breakfast table:

> *Bless the food before us,*
> *the family beside us,*
> *and the love between us.*
> *Amen.*

"James and Tresa — or whoever lived here last — sure loved signs with lame expressions," Ichiro said. He forced a laugh, trying to lighten the mood.

Jacob didn't respond. The signs might have been homey when the house had been lived in, but now they felt unsettling.

Ichiro shrugged and said, "Let's move on. This kitchen stinks."

Jacob nodded, eager to put the whole situation behind them. They exited the kitchen through a different door and found themselves back in the front hall. There was a door that led to the east wing of the house, but it was locked. Without pausing to wonder what was concealed behind it, Jacob moved down the hall to the next door. It swung open when he pushed on it, so he and Ichiro entered the room.

It was filled with mismatched furniture that seemed odd and disjointed: large antique office furniture (a desk, a chair and a wooden filing cabinet) and baby furniture (a crib, a changing table, a rocking chair). Behind the crib was a closed door. The wooden walls had been painted shades of light blue. Perhaps the oddest item was a medical skeleton that stood on a pole near the door, and there was yet another framed motto on the wall:

Let them sleep,
for when they wake
they will move mountains.

Jacob felt more uncomfortable with every passing second spent in the house.

"This is the weirdest baby's room ever," Ichiro said. He sat in the office chair. It groaned and squealed, a grating sound that dug into Jacob's eardrums and made him wince. "This desk is old, man. Like, super old. Even older than most of the junk you see out at the flea market." He tried to open the drawers but they were locked shut. He swivelled the chair around and it screeched loudly again.

"Cut it out," Jacob pleaded.

"Sorry." He stood up and crossed the room, where he examined a picture frame that leaned against the wall. He picked it up and looked closely at it. "Hey, check it out. It's a medical diploma. Speaking of the flea market, I wonder if I could sell this to someone out there."

Jacob peered over Ichiro's shoulder at the old certificate written in elegant script on yellowed paper.

Trinity Medical College

in affiliation with
The University of Trinity College,
The University of Toronto,
Queen's University and The University of Manitoba,
know all Men by these present that

James Aaron Stockwell

has been deliberately examined in the several branches of
Medical Science by the Faculty of Trinity Medical College
and has satisfied them that he is qualified to practise
Medicine, Surgery and Midwifery and entitled to receive
this Diploma issued under the authority of the
Act of Legislature of Ontario incorporating the College.

James Aaron Stockwell

is also hereby admitted a fellow by Examination of
Trinity Medical College.
Given under our hands and under the Seal of the
Corporation on this the

26th day of May 1899

Thomas Harrington, Dean

A dozen names and titles followed the Dean's name, running down to the bottom of the diploma.

"So the guy with the beard in the photograph, James Stockwell, was a doctor," Jacob said. "Explains the skeleton, and how they afforded such a big house on their own private island. But it doesn't explain why it's been empty ever since they died."

"How can you be sure no one else has lived here since the Stockwells?"

"There's no modern furniture, no TV, nothing that seems to have been made after, like, the early 1900s. Just a bunch of antique stuff, a black-and-white photograph dated 1906 and a medical diploma from 1899. And a phonograph."

"With a German record in it," Ichiro said. Then he added, "Not that that's helpful to add."

"Maybe it's not completely useless. Tresa sounds like a German name. We can probably assume that the record was hers."

Ichiro laughed. "You're being generous. It was a pointless observation."

Jacob shrugged and offered a sheepish half smile. "Yeah, it was pretty pointless."

"I might not be as good at the sleuthing as you are, but this is really fun."

"It's like our very own escape room with a mystery

to solve and the added benefit that we're not actually locked in."

"And it doesn't cost anything to play." Ichiro offered a fist and Jacob bumped it with his own. "Boom."

Tee-hee-hee.

Jacob flinched and felt his entire body — every muscle — tense up.

It was the trilling, carefree sound of a boy's laughter. Such a happy sound under normal circumstances, but it wasn't a happy sound here, and certainly not now. It had come from behind the door that was blocked by the baby's crib.

Worse than the sound was the realization that it hadn't been created by his imagination; it was real. Ichiro had also jumped and cursed, and he was also now staring at the crib, wide-eyed and horrified.

"You heard that too?" Jacob asked breathlessly.

"Yeah, I heard it," Ichiro said. "Help me move the crib."

"Are you crazy?"

"It sounded like a kid. We have to check."

"No way."

"Jake, if there's a kid back there he's probably trapped. We can't just sit here and do nothing. We have to help." Ichiro crossed the room and put his hands on the crib.

"Are you sure you want to go through that door?"

Jacob asked slowly. "Maybe it's been blocked for a reason." *Or, if someone's trapped, why are they laughing?* He decided to keep that question to himself.

"Are you going to help me or not?" Ichiro asked, sounding exasperated.

Jacob didn't move. His feet felt like they had been frozen to the ground.

"Fine," Ichiro said. He pushed the crib away from the wall, enough to open the door and slip through. Before he disappeared from sight he said, "Stay here and do nothing if you want."

And then he was gone.

Jacob's blood pumped through his veins as his heartbeat filled his ears with an odd, pounding rhythm: *Boom-boom boom. Boom-boom boom. Boom-boom boom boom, boom-boom-boom.*

He rubbed his face, steadied his breathing, and then did something that surprised him: he freed his feet and followed. It was better than waiting alone.

The windows in the barricaded room had been blacked out, making it even darker than the rest of the house. He couldn't see Ichiro, nor much of anything else.

"Ichiro?" Jacob said, with a quiver in his voice. "You in here?"

A whisper from the far corner of the room: "Yes."

Jacob looked in the direction of the voice. His eyes slowly adjusted to the darkness. Not enough to make out every detail, but enough to see a shadowy figure that he assumed was Ichiro. He was sitting on something low to the ground, still as a statue.

The floor squeaked as Jacob crossed to his friend.

Ichiro raised his hands at Jacob. "Don't come any closer," he hissed. "You'll scare him off." After a moment that felt like it stretched out to the length of an eternity, Ichiro added in a whisper, "He's right behind you."

Before Jacob could ask Ichiro who was behind him, the sound of music, punctuated by crackling hisses, drifted toward them from the other side of the house. From the parlour.

"The phonograph," Jacob said. *It works. But who's playing it?*

Even though Jacob didn't understand the lyrics — the recording was of a woman singing operatically in German — the song was instantly familiar. A classic lullaby his mother had sung to him when he was a child.

The sound of feet travelled across the room. Jacob followed the sound but didn't see anyone pass.

Ichiro stood. Jacob realized his friend had been sitting on the edge of an old cot, one of a dozen he now saw lined both sides of the room (*Let them sleep* popped into his head). Ichiro followed the sound of the phantom feet toward another closed door. Nail holes lined the door frame. On the ground were scattered two-by-four boards with bent nails sticking out of them.

Before Ichiro reached the door, it flew open on its own and slammed against the wall with a loud clap.

Ichiro looked down — the open doorway revealed a set of rickety stairs leading to the basement. "Stay back!" he yelled.

Jacob disregarded the command and ran to Ichiro's side.

The stairs leading down were thin and warped. The walls in the basement below were crudely assembled with brick, mortar, wooden boards and patches of cement. The floor was dirt. There appeared to be little headspace, less than two metres from ground to ceiling. A pungent waft of earth and mould and something else — something metallic — rolled up from the depths of the house.

The sound of the phantom footsteps hurried down the stairs, followed by a scurrying noise that sounded to Jacob like a scavenger running away after being spotted.

There was whispering from below, muffled but urgent. It sounded like there was more than one voice, but how many? Two? Three? More? They overlapped and twisted into a coil like a ball of snakes, one nearly indistinguishable from the other.

The whispering stopped. The phonograph's lullaby ended.

And then, after a pregnant pause, the screaming in the basement began.

FIVE

July 16

There's an art to walking silently on crushed gravel in baseball cleats. Glove at the ready, Jacob crept toward third base without alerting the runner, a kid named Sebastien, who had taken a good three-stride lead toward home plate.

Sebastien was crouched low to the ground like a coiled spring, his fingers twitching and dangling between his legs a few centimetres above the gravel. He didn't see Jacob — his eyes were focused on Hannah with hawk-like intensity.

As a lefty, she stood on the pitcher's mound with her back to third base. Jacob spotted her sneak a quick glance over her shoulder, aware of the potential to pick the runner off and end the game with another victory. She was the Tigers' best player and possessed a hyper-awareness of everything that was happening across the diamond at all times.

Without warning, Hannah suddenly swivelled and fired a blistering throw toward third.

Jacob caught the ball — a little high — and dropped his glove to tag Sebastien, but too late. Sebastien slid under and touched the base with his hand. Safe.

"Not gonna get me that easy," Sebastien said, grinning up at Jacob from the ground.

"And you're not going to score a run that easy, not with her closing," Jacob said. He tossed the ball back to Hannah and stepped away from the base. It would have been nice to pick off Sebastien and win the game, but Jacob was happy that he caught the ball at all. He'd already made two big fielding errors earlier in the game and had batted 0 for 3, having struck out twice and grounded out once. His head wasn't fully in the game. How could it be? In the days since he and Ichiro had run away from Summer's End and canoed home as fast as they could, he'd thought about little else than what had happened there — the sound of laughter and footsteps followed by whispers and screams, not to mention the phonograph that played on its own. The lullaby had filled Jacob's head in a nearly continuous loop for five days. In the swirling mess of his mind, he could hardly concentrate on anything else.

And despite the fear he felt when he thought of Summer's End, something was calling him back.

Jacob shook his head as if he could toss the memories out of his mind the way a dog shakes water off its back. He had a baseball game to win. He needed to focus.

To his left, playing shortstop, Ichiro called out some encouragement. "Let's go, Tigers. Strike the batter out, Hannah." He didn't seem to be as preoccupied as Jacob was with what had happened in the old house. He always had an easier time letting things go and moving on. Jacob wished he could live as carefree as Ichiro appeared.

Hannah held her glove in front of her chin and fiddled with the concealed ball, getting her fingers in just the right spot for her next pitch. Jacob couldn't see what she had in store, but he had a pretty good idea. He assumed the batter could probably predict what type of pitch was coming next too, since he knew Hannah better than anyone else on either team.

Standing tense at the plate, bat raised above his right shoulder, was Hayden.

He'd been upset earlier in the month when they'd found out Jacob, Ichiro and Hannah had all been placed on the Tigers and he'd been placed on the Athletics. And now here he was, facing off against his sister. In the ninth inning. Down by one with the tying run on third. The count was two balls, two strikes.

With two strikes on the board, Hannah always went with her knuckleball. After a couple of fastballs and a curve or two, she knew batters were eager to swing, and the knuckleball took full advantage of that. It was a deceiving pitch.

Hannah continued to fiddle with the ball. The afternoon sun baked Jacob's skin. He wiped sweat from his eyes. *C'mon, Hannah*, he thought impatiently. *If he didn't know you were setting up to throw a knuckler before, he does now.*

She stole one more glance over her shoulder at Sebastien, dropped her arms, then took a powerful stride toward home and threw the last pitch of the game.

A heater.

Hayden didn't swing. Expecting a knuckler, he watched the ball fly past his waist in a straight line, right down the middle, before he could wrap his head around what had happened.

"Stee-rike three!" the umpire shouted as he pointed two fingers toward the home team's bench.

The Tigers cheered and Hannah pumped her fist in the air. Jacob clapped and walked to the mound to congratulate Hannah.

"What was that, Hayden?"

Jacob stopped and turned. It was Sebastien pacing toward home plate, his cheeks blood red. He tore off his batting glove and threw it in the dirt. "She served it up and you didn't even swing!"

Hayden stood beside the plate, staring down at his cleats, as if he couldn't believe what had happened.

He looked up at Sebastien, his teammate, but didn't answer.

"Hey, man," Jacob said. "Calm down. It's just a game."

Sebastien didn't pay attention to Jacob. "You're gonna lose us a lot of games this season, aren't you? Figures I'd get stuck on a team with *you*."

Hayden finally found his voice, or maybe he just heard Sebastien's taunts for the first time. "I feel the same about you," he said.

"Me?" Sebastien laughed. It was a sound like a question mark, punctuated by disbelief and rounded out by anger. "I'm not the one who lost the game. I'm not the one who got struck out by a *girl*." He picked up his pace and barrelled toward Hayden.

But he didn't reach him.

With a few long strides Hannah caught up to Sebastien and grabbed the back of his collar. She pulled him backwards, hard. His eyes bulged in shock as his jersey dug into his neck and she dragged him down to the gravel.

Hannah dropped a knee onto his chest as dust swirled around her head. "Look at that," she said, raising a clenched fist. "*You* are the one who got struck by a girl."

The gravity of the situation washed over Jacob like a cold wave. He and Ichiro pulled Hannah off

Sebastien and stopped her from pummelling him. She didn't resist. She'd made her point, but the damage was done.

Sebastien rolled onto his side, fetal position, and coughed. His coach helped him up off the ground while the Tigers' coach looked gravely at Hannah.

The umpire tried to keep his voice from rising, but he was clearly flustered. "Go home, Hannah," he said. "You're automatically suspended from the next game."

"That's not fair!" Hannah protested. "Sebastien was going to—"

"It doesn't matter one bit what Sebastien was or wasn't about to do," he interrupted, "because he didn't do it. You're the only player who fought. The rules state that's an automatic one-game suspension, and the league will review what happened to determine if you should be suspended longer or removed from the league altogether. Now, leave the field immediately." He pointed to the parking lot.

With pinched lips and fire in her eyes, Hannah stormed off the field. She threw her glove to the ground, scooped it back up and biked away alone.

"She's mad," Ichiro said.

"No kidding," Jacob said. He scanned the field, the bleachers and the surrounding area for Hayden.

His bike, Jacob noticed, was gone. He'd snuck off in the commotion of the one-sided fight and Hannah's ejection.

Jacob didn't blame Hayden for leaving without waiting for anyone else. If Jacob had been struck out by his sister and then saved from a fight by her, he'd probably want to disappear too. For a day or two, at least. Maybe a month.

Maybe a summer.

———

Speed and wind. Jacob smiled. He closed his eyes for a moment and enjoyed the sun bathing his face and the air blowing past. It was so freeing coasting down a steep hill, his wheels spinning wildly without pedalling. He became one with his bike, his hands melded with the rubber handles, his blood pumping with each revolution of the tires, his heart ringing like a bell. He forgot about the baseball game and the fight that ended it. He forgot about the twins, each likely upset for very different reasons.

He even forgot about the things — whatever they were — in the basement of Summer's End.

Ichiro coasted behind him, the rainbow-coloured Spokey Dokeys on his wheels *clicking* and *clacking* like fireworks. When Ichiro bought them at a garage sale,

Jacob had told him that Spokey Dokeys were for little kids. Ichiro didn't care. He did his own thing. It was, Jacob felt, one of his best qualities. Jacob almost wanted to buy some Spokey Dokeys of his own.

They made a sharp left turn onto Main Street and biked through town, zigzagging around parked cars and summer tourists. People sitting at patio tables watched them pass. A small white dog yipped and chased them for a block before its owner caught up and leashed it. Luckily they didn't pass Colton's mother.

Near the edge of town the boys approached East Road Convenience, an old two-storey building with wood-slat walls painted lime green. It was the only place in town to buy a comic book, a pack of baseball cards and a bagful of candy in one stop.

"Hey, let's pull in here," Ichiro said. "Do you want some ice cream? Or a drink?"

Jacob's cheeks flushed. He patted his baseball uniform's pants pockets to show they were empty. "I left my wallet at home."

"Don't worry," Ichiro said, pulling out his wallet. "I'll pay."

"Thanks, man!"

A bell dinged when they opened the door. The old man who worked there emerged from a backroom and walked through a narrow aisle packed with junk food, making his way slowly to the front counter. He was tall, lanky and wore his shoulder-length grey hair in a ponytail. Perched on his bony nose was a pair of large tinted glasses. Jacob had never seen anyone else working the cash. Jacob and his friends called him The Willow, but never to the old man's face.

"How many times I tell you kids not to come in here with cleats on?" The Willow asked, gum smacking in his mouth between every other word. His tone was more resigned than angry. He sounded tired. He always sounded tired. "You're gonna damage my floors."

"Sorry," Jacob said, with an apologetic shrug. Neither he nor Ichiro took off their cleats. The Willow waved his hand and grunted as he half sat, half leaned on the stool behind the counter.

The boys wandered the aisles, passing the bins of bulk candy and racks filled with comic books. Jacob lingered there for a moment and studied the cover of an X-Men comic. Professor X sat in the foreground with his head slumped, while Wolverine, Cyclops, Storm and a few other mutant superheroes stood with bowed heads in the shadows behind their leader. A caption screamed "DEATH . . . TO THE X-MEN!" He flipped through the pages, put it back on the rack, and then joined Ichiro at the fridge. Ichiro grabbed a bottle of cream soda. Jacob picked orange pop.

Ichiro stopped in front of a chest freezer, slid its glass door open and reached inside. He pulled out two ice-cream bars. "You want one?"

Jacob shook his head. "Nah. Just the drink is fine."

Ichiro tossed one of the ice creams back into the freezer. He paid — The Willow handed over his change without any further remarks — and they stepped outside.

"Huh," Ichiro said, studying the change in his hand.

"What's up?"

"I think The Willow shortchanged me. Wait here. I'll be right back."

East Road Convenience, with an unpaved dirt parking lot and exterior walls that had only ever been cleaned by the rain, was no building to lean against. Jacob walked his bike to the street and let it fall on the grass beside the sidewalk. He sat on the curb. He didn't need to wait long before Ichiro exited the store and joined him.

Ichiro unwrapped his ice-cream bar and Jacob took a drink of orange pop. It fizzed on his tongue and burned the back of his throat in the best possible way.

"How are you feeling?" Ichiro asked.

Jacob glanced sideways at his friend. "I'm fine."

"Just fine?"

With a furrowed brow, Jacob nodded. Ichiro was up

to something, he just couldn't guess what.

Ichiro smiled. "The sun is shining, you're sipping orange pop, you've got the latest *Uncanny X-Men* to look forward to reading and you're telling me you're just *fine*?"

Jacob laughed. "I don't have the latest—"

Ichiro reached behind his back and pulled an X-Men comic out from under his shirt. He handed it to Jacob. "I saw you eyeing it in the store so I got it when I went back inside."

"Wait. Was the whole 'The Willow shortchanged me' thing just an act?"

Ichiro shrugged and smiled.

"Wow. You shouldn't have."

"I'm not giving it to you, if that's what you're thinking. I want it back, but you can read it first."

"Thank you." Jacob didn't know what else to say. It was a small gesture of friendship, but it meant a lot to Jacob, more than Ichiro could have known.

A warm breeze fluttered the comic's pages. The boys watched cars drive past and birds fly overhead. The idle chatter of some grown-ups drifted toward them from The Wet Whistle, a pub with a lively patio that shared the parking lot with East Road Convenience.

Ichiro spoke first. "How long do you think Hannah will be suspended?"

"I don't know. She didn't hit Sebastien, so maybe the league will go easy on her." Jacob wondered what the twins were doing at that moment. They were probably in their rooms, silently stewing. Jacob took another sip of pop.

Ichiro licked the final smear of ice cream off the bar's wooden stick and tossed it in the dirt next to an ant mound. Ants swarmed the stick immediately. "I wonder what their dad's going to say to Hannah when he finds out."

Jacob watched the ants climb over one another in a frenzy, their tiny antennae and mandibles quivering. He didn't like talking about Hayden and Hannah's home life, so he held his tongue. *If you can't say anything positive*, his mother was fond of telling him, *don't say anything at all*.

"Their father gives me a bad vibe," Ichiro continued. "Every time I go there it feels more like a prison than a home. If he was my father, I think I'd rather have no father at all."

The words stung Jacob. He set his pop bottle down on the street and closed his eyes. "Trust me, having any kind of dad is better than having none." But even as he said it, he wondered if it was true. Would he rather have Hayden's father than no father?

"Sorry, Jacob, I didn't mean—"

He held up his hand and forced a smile. "Don't worry about it. I know."

Ichiro nodded. "So, are we going to talk about Summer's End?"

The question came so far out of left field that Jacob knew Ichiro must have been dying to ask it all day.

"Whatever we heard race through the main floor and down the basement stairs freaked the heck out of me," Ichiro said, without waiting for Jacob to answer his question. "But the crazy thing is I kind of want to go back. Is that nuts?"

Jacob shook his head. "No, that's not nuts. I do too."

Ichiro exhaled loudly, as if he'd been holding his breath, and pulled his knees to his chest.

"I can't stop thinking about the place," Jacob continued. "That's why my game was off today. The sounds we heard — the laughter and footsteps and screams — they're playing in an endless loop in my head along with that lullaby we heard coming from the phonograph. How did it start playing on its own?"

Ichiro shrugged. "Maybe . . . I dunno, maybe the bunny hopped against it or something."

"You really believe that?"

Ichiro shook his head. "No."

"Whatever's going on, I have this feeling, like a sixth sense, that there's something we're meant to do there."

Ichiro nodded. "Me too. It's like a scab I can't resist picking."

"Gross."

"Yeah, but also apt," Ichiro said.

"Well, we shouldn't go back blindly. We need to find out everything and anything we can about the Stockwells and their house first." Jacob took out his phone and opened a browser. Ichiro did the same. They typed varying combinations of key search words:

"Valeton"

"Sepequoi Lake"

"Doctor Stockwell"

"Summer's End"

"You getting anything?" Ichiro asked.

Jacob shook his head. "No. Lists of Muskoka doctors, but no Stockwell. A Valeton tourism site that encourages people to spend their summer vacation here. Some company that makes music gear. A bunch of books, movies and games named *Summer's End*. A sad little Wikipedia entry for the town of Valeton. Nothing else, really."

"Me too."

"Let's go home and call it a night," Jacob said, as he stood, tucked the X-Men comic book under the waist of his pants and swung a leg over his bike. He checked the time on his phone — it was getting late and his mother would have dinner on the table soon. "We can meet downtown tomorrow. I know a place where we might be able to find obscure local history like this."

"Oh yeah? Where?"

"Where else? The library."

SIX

July 17

Specks of sunlit dust danced above rows of bookshelves. The library was old — the building had originally been the town's first general store and trading post — but it was also huge. An extension had been built on the west wing, and the librarians seemed grimly determined to pack as many books into the library as was physically possible. The shelving had been arranged in a zigzagging, haphazard fashion that created a spider's web of hidden spaces and dead ends. Only three or four people were ever working at a time, and most of the librarians were happy to leave Jacob alone. It was his favourite place in town to get lost for a few hours. The seclusion the library offered was so absolute that he often wondered how long it would take for his body to be discovered should some tragedy befall him — a stack of books falling and pinning him to the ground, for example. Maybe hours. Maybe days.

Most of the time, Jacob read comics and old paperback novels — fantasy, sci-fi and horror — on a bench in a bay window on the second floor. But he and Ichiro had come on a mission.

The library was mostly empty. A couple of high-school students who worked there chatted idly in the Careers section, ignoring the carts of books they were supposed to be shelving and failing to see the irony in the area they had selected to waste some time. An old man napped in a soft chair in a dark corner, his snores mixing with the strands of music playing through his headset. How he had fallen asleep with the volume turned up so high, Jacob couldn't guess. A young mother with a baby in her arms chased after three-year-old twins who were whacking each other with books. And a group of ten-year-olds crowded around the reference desk, digging through a treasure chest filled with dollar store prizes, while the man who worked there made some personal recommendations.

"If I were you," he said in a mild English accent, "I would dig a little deeper. I believe you'll find some Pokémon cards and Monster High tattoos stashed down there."

The kids squealed with delight when they found something worth getting excited about and happily moved on.

"Jacob," the man said jovially, when he saw the boys waiting in line. "Good to see you again."

"Good to see you too, Rio."

"Sorry about the wait. Those kids were claiming

some prizes for the summer reading club. It's a mad house in here. Simply mad."

The old man in the corner snored so loudly he woke himself up, but then he rubbed his nose, smacked his lips three times and promptly fell back asleep.

Ichiro looked over his shoulder at the old man and back to Rio. "Yeah. This place is a zoo."

"I'm sorry, I don't believe we've met."

"This is my friend Ichiro," Jacob said.

"And do you have a library card, Jacob's friend Ichiro?"

Ichiro glanced at Jacob for direction. Jacob shrugged. "Um, no?" Ichiro said.

"Security!" Rio shouted.

Jacob jumped. The old man sputtered awake and looked from side to side wildly. Ichiro looked panicked. "What?" he said. "Am I seriously in trouble?"

"No, of course not." Rio laughed. "I just wanted an excuse to wake up Frank over there. His snoring has been driving me nuts for the better part of an hour."

"You crazy loon," Frank shouted across the floor.

"Go back to sleep, Frank. I'll wake you when it's time to close up and go home."

Frank waved his hand and muttered something incomprehensible, then closed his eyes. He was snoring again within seconds.

It had taken Ichiro a bit of time to fully understand what had just happened, but once he realized that he wasn't going to be kicked out of the library for not having a card he chuckled a little. "Good one. You got me."

"I got Frank too," Rio said, with a mischievous grin. "You have to find a little fun wherever you can. So, how can I help you two gentlemen?"

"We're hoping you might have some old copies of the *Valeton Voice*," Jacob said.

"But of course," Rio said dramatically, as if he thought of his desk as his personal stage. "What sort of a library would we be if we didn't collect and store our very own town's history?"

"Not a very good one, I'm guessing," Ichiro said.

"Right you are, Ichiro. Right you are." Rio peered at Jacob from across the reference desk. "I must say, this is a change. You haven't outgrown superheroes already, have you?" He was one of the few librarians who had bothered to learn Jacob's name — they had a shared interest in comics.

Familiar with the library's schedule and aware that Rio would be working, Jacob knew this would be the perfect day for the task at hand. He expected Rio to question him a little, but also buy just about anything he'd say, so Jacob had come prepared with an answer. "Of course not. It's for a summer school project." He hooked a thumb at Ichiro. "We were paired up and told to find a newspaper article in the *Valeton Voice* from the early 1900s, and then present it to the class with some observations about the time period."

"Summer school?" Rio said, surprised. "I didn't think you'd need to retake any classes, Jacob."

"I don't," Jacob lied easily. "I'm working ahead for extra credit."

"Me too," Ichiro added with a smile. "We're smart."

Rio stood and walked out from behind the desk, leading the boys through the library. "Ah. I see. Well, I'm relieved to hear you're not done with comics. The stats from all your checkouts is one of the main reasons I can justify keeping them in the collection, and it took me too many years to convince the board we should have them in the first place." They entered the local history room, a small and cozy room with a fireplace, a leather chair, a microfilm reader and one computer. A metal filing cabinet was shoved into a corner, and the shelves were crammed with books on the Muskoka region and binders of council meeting notes and other assorted items of local interest. On the wall above the computer hung a large framed photograph of the Queen. There didn't seem to be much order to the room's contents, but Rio knew it like the back of his hand. He unlocked the bottom drawer of the filing cabinet and asked, "Do you know what year you need to search?"

Jacob nodded. "We were assigned 1906." It was the year James and Tresa were married, and as good a place as any that Jacob could think to start.

"I've got good news and bad news. Which do you want first?"

"Um, the good news?"

"The *Valeton Voice* published its first paper in 1903. If your teacher had assigned you a year earlier than that, you wouldn't have been able to complete the assignment. But you're in luck — you get to do your homework!"

"Yay," Ichiro said, trying his best to sell his delivery.

"And the bad news?" Jacob asked.

"I've been spending the past few summers digitizing the collection, scanning every page of every newspaper and putting them online so they're easily searchable, even from home. But I'm going back in time, and I've only made it to 1955. So you're going to have to scan through reels of microfilm." Rio ran his fingers along a row of small boxes that sat in the drawer. "1903, 1904, 1905 . . . here we go . . . 1906." He pulled out four boxes, each one labelled with the year and a three-month range. He opened the box labelled *1906, Jan. to Mar.*, unpacked a reel of film and wound it into the reader.

The microfilm reader was large and bulky. It consisted of a big, boxy screen that sat above a lamp, reels and a few different buttons and knobs. Although it was probably built in the last forty or fifty years, it looked like something from the age of the dinosaurs.

Looks like it weighs as much as a Mack Truck, Jacob thought, wondering how the wooden table it rested on hadn't cracked under its weight.

A lamp lit the reel and projected the first page of the *Valeton Voice* onto the screen. Rio gave Jacob and Ichiro a quick lesson on how to operate the machine, made sure they knew what they were doing and then turned to leave. He paused just outside the door. "Guess I'm going to be teaching a lot of kids how to do that in the days ahead."

"What?" Jacob said.

"Operate the reader. You know, because of your assignment. I assume you two aren't the only ones in summer school who have to complete it, right?"

"Oh, yeah. Right."

"Okay, then. The next three 1906 reels are there on the table if you need them. I'll leave the cabinet unlocked. Do me a favour and put them back when you're done. You know where to find me if you require any more assistance."

Once they were alone, Ichiro said, "He's going to

wonder what happened when no one else comes in to use the microfilm reader."

Jacob shrugged. "We'll cross that bridge when we get there. Right now, all I care about is trying to find out what happened to the Stockwells, and why Summer's End has been empty and neglected for so long." He placed his fingers on the dial and rotated it. Images of newspaper pages from January 1906 scrolled left to right. They scanned the article titles for anything that might be linked to Summer's End or the Stockwells. There were marriage notices, but not one for James and Tresa. They scanned headlines for any mention of Sepequoi Lake, but still nothing caught their eye. Day by day, week by week, month by month, all they found were reports about local agriculture, politics and small-town events. Jacob's back and neck were sore by the time they had finished the first reel of the year. He removed it from the reader, set up the reel from the box labelled *1906, Apr. to Jun.*, stretched his spine and dove back in.

As pages zipped by, an article caught Jacob's attention and he stopped. The word *hospital* had jumped out, so he pointed to the screen and he and Ichiro read for a moment in silence.

ASSISTANCE NEEDED FOR MUSKOKA FREE HOSPITAL FOR CONSUMPTIVES

The Muskoka Free Hospital for Consumptives has cured many patients afflicted by tuberculosis. Since this institution opened in Gravenhurst more than three years ago, 560 patients have been cared for. Not a single applicant has ever been refused admission to the Muskoka Free Hospital for Consumptives due to his or her poverty.

Within the previous month accommodation has been increased by twenty-five beds, adding to the burdens of maintenance, but in the faith that a generous public will come to the aid of the trustees.

Contributions may be sent to W.J. Gage, Esq., Osgoode Hall, Toronto.

"What's tuberculosis?" Ichiro asked.

"It's a contagious disease that affects the lungs. It can be fatal but I think it's not as serious in North America as it used to be, like, a hundred years ago."

"How do you know this stuff?"

"I read," Jacob said, deadpan. "You should try it sometime."

"Hey, I read!"

"Cereal boxes don't count."

Ichiro didn't miss a beat: "But there's some fascinating information printed on them. For example, did you know that Cocoa Krispies now helps support your child's immunity? It's true! According to the box."

"You know they can claim just about anything they want to on the box, right?"

"Sure, just don't tell my mom that."

"My lips are sealed." Jacob turned to face the microfilm reader again. "Back to the reason we're here. This article didn't mention Dr. Stockwell, so let's move on."

April ended. May came and went. June wound down, and they had skimmed their way through half the year but had nothing to show for it.

Ichiro sighed. "Is it possible they didn't get married in 1906? Maybe someone put the wrong year on the back of that photo. Or maybe their wedding wasn't published in the paper."

"Maybe. But what do we do? Go through every single year? I wouldn't have the patience for that, especially since we're already looking for a needle in a haystack, and that needle might not even exist."

"Do you want to stop and go home? You can come over to my house for dinner. My mother's making a traditional Japanese dinner."

"Maybe," Jacob said. Ichiro's parents were great

cooks, but Jacob's mother would be getting off work soon and he didn't want to leave her alone with such short notice. He pointed to the last two boxes, labelled 1906, *Jul. to Sept.* and 1906, *Oct. to Dec.*

"Let's just go through these first. I want to do it now while we've got them. Once Rio starts to question the story we gave him, we might not have another opportunity without raising suspicion."

Ichiro sighed and slumped in his seat. "All right. One more hour, max."

Jacob caught on to the pattern the newspapers followed from issue to issue. Local news in the front, entertainment and sports in the middle and classifieds and town gossip in the back. He flew through each issue and stopped on the classifieds, scanned the marriage notices for the Stockwells' names, and then, when he didn't find anything relevant, he flew to the back of the next issue. Scroll, search, strike out, repeat.

Ichiro grew bored and used Jacob's library card to log on to the computer. He checked a couple of social media sites, looked up the baseball scores and played a few online games. "What was the name of the record in Summer's End? The German one?"

Jacob pulled his gaze away from the microfilm reader, thankful for the break, and tried to recall. "It started with the letter W. Wiggenlead, or something like that.

The two words I definitely remember under the title were 'guten' and 'nacht.'"

Ichiro typed those two words into the search engine and hit return. "You were right, they're German for 'good' and 'night.'" He then searched for "wiggenlead guten nacht." Google corrected his spelling and displayed a parade of results. "You were close. It says here it's 'Wiegenlied: Guten Abend, gute Nacht.' In English it's known as 'Brahms' Lullaby: Good Evening, Good Night,' or the 'Cradle Song.'" Ichiro clicked on one of the search results. "Wikipedia says it's one of the most famous melodies in the world. Check it out: they have an embedded audio clip." He hit the play arrow and sat back as muffled crackling sounds hissed out of the speakers.

It was slow and sad, soothing and melancholic. The music pulsed through the speakers and seemed to fill the small room with icy blue waves of electricity that made the afternoon feel dark and suffocating. It was a different recording but the same song that had played from the phonograph.

Lullaby and good night,
With roses bedight,
With lilies o'er spread
Is baby's wee bed.
Lay thee down now and rest,
May thy slumber be blessed.

Lullaby and good night,
Thy mother's delight,
Bright angels beside
My darling abide.
They will guard thee at rest,
Thou shalt wake on my breast.

The music ended, and after a brief moment of static hiss, the recording stopped and the room fell deafeningly quiet.

"My mom used to sing that to me when I was little," Jacob said. His thoughts ebbed and flowed, from his mother, to the calming sound of the lake lapping against the canoe as if calling him to the island, to the old phonograph and family quotes in Summer's End.

Family
Where life begins
and love never ends . . .

Family is everything.

Bless the food before us,
the family beside us,
and the love between us.
Amen.

Let them sleep,
for when they wake
they will move mountains.

Other than the last one, each of the expressions specifically mentioned family. And Jacob assumed the last one must refer to sleeping children.

"The Stockwells must have had kids," he said.

"Huh?"

"The lullaby in the phonograph, the family quotes in every room, the crib . . ." *pushed up against the door*, Jacob thought.

"The sound of children whispering in the basement," Ichiro added. "But if they were such a happy family, why did those whispers turn to screams? Why had the basement door been nailed shut at some point?"

"I don't know," Jacob said. He had a feeling he didn't *want* to know the answers to those particular questions. He couldn't think of anything else to say, so he turned back to the microfilm reader and resumed scrolling through days long past.

He was in the middle of August when Ichiro sat up suddenly and told Jacob to stop.

"What?" Jacob asked, his interest piqued.

"Go back a bit. I think I saw something."

Jacob's heartbeat sped up. He flexed his sore fingers

and turned the dial in the opposite direction. The pages passed slowly from right to left.

Ichiro's eyes darted over the screen, searching for whatever he thought he might have seen. "There!" he shouted, tapping the screen in triumph. "Right there."

It wasn't a simple marriage notice. It was a full article, and Jacob felt like they had hit the jackpot.

DOCTOR BUILDS
DREAM HOUSE

The Town of Valeton can boast one of the most beautiful private residences in the Muskoka Region — perhaps north of the City of Toronto. It is in process of completion by Dr. James A. Stockwell, previously a surgeon at Toronto General and currently Doctor of Medicine at the Muskoka Free Hospital for Consumptives in nearby Gravenhurst. Construction of the home was commenced two years ago last spring, and was to have been ready for occupation in three years; but, we are told, it is now expected to be completed by the first of December, some three or four months earlier than contracted. Destined as it is to be the leading architectural ornament of the town, and so far as private residences are concerned, the leading one of the region, some description of it must prove of interest to our readers, local as well as distant.

In the fashion of a country cottage, the house has been constructed primarily of wood, but it is no mere summer home, for it has been built to be habitable year round, and includes a basement dug nearly six feet below ground level. Perhaps the crowning achievement of the property is rightfully the property itself, for the house occupies a private island on Sepequoi Lake that is breathtaking in its natural beauty and majesty.

Our readers will readily judge that such an immense structure could not be erected and finished in such a remote location without a corresponding outlay of capital. The property, including the building, has already cost Dr. Stockwell the sum of $11,000. But the actual cost of the house when finished will not be less than $13,000, to say nothing of the money that will be necessary to furnish in a suitable style the numerous magnificent rooms.

Dr. Stockwell, who has dedicated his life's work to the treatment of consumptives, and his fiancee Tresa Althaus have named the house "Summer's End" in the English tradition of designating a private residence of suitable worth and grandeur. They plan to wed in fall of this year, and Miss Althaus

desires to fill their home with
the pitter-patter of little feet
and laughter of small children
with all due speed, God willing.
Our readers will surely wish them
well on this grand adventure on
which they are about to embark.

"Hoo boy," Ichiro said once they had finished reading. "Thirteen thousand dollars. I think my family's flight to Japan cost that much."

"So now we know that the Stockwells not only lived in Summer's End," Jacob said, "but that they built it too. And James treated tuberculosis patients in Gravenhurst." It was an odd coincidence, Jacob thought, that they had chanced on an article about the Muskoka Free Hospital for Consumptives. But then again, if it was over crowded during an epidemic, he assumed there would have been regular pleas in the paper for assistance and donations. There were probably articles about the hospital in every other edition. He must have missed them.

"And look at that," Ichiro said. He pointed to the bottom of the article and read aloud. "'They plan to wed in fall of this year, and Miss Althaus desires to fill their home with the pitter-patter of little feet and laughter of small children with all due speed, God willing.' Tresa was baby crazy. You were right, once again."

Just this once, Jacob wished he had been wrong. He had a feeling that something bad — something sinister — had happened to the Stockwells' children.

SEVEN

July 23

The mid-afternoon sun, swollen and bright, dominated the cloudless sky. Its heat radiated upon the earth, drying the grass yellow and burning anyone caught outdoors too long.

Jacob and Ichiro sat in the shade of a tall elm tree, fanning themselves with their ball caps and trying to keep cool. Although they had both walked off the basketball court more than ten minutes before, sweat continued to bead on their foreheads and run down their necks.

"Man, it's hot," Ichiro said

"That's the understatement of the century," Jacob said.

"I feel like I should be sitting on a rocking chair, mopping my brow with my pocket handkerchief and speaking in a southern accent."

"While sipping a sarsaparilla."

"I've always wondered what sarsaparilla is."

"I have no idea," Jacob said. "But it sounds delicious."

They were too hot to laugh. Instead, Ichiro laid back and closed his eyes, and Jacob pinched his shirt near his collar and pulled it back and forth rapidly to create a little airflow around his neck. Insects buzzed loudly from their cool hiding places under blades of grass and within folds of tree bark.

"I don't even care that I got knocked out so early," Ichiro said. "Better to be soundly beaten and horribly embarrassed than to die of heatstroke, that's my motto."

"Words to live by." Jacob idly watched the game of HORSE through half-closed eyes. Clear, shimmering heat waves radiated off the cracked asphalt, giving the basketball court the appearance of a desert mirage.

Hannah stood at half court, eyeing the net, the ball clutched in her hands. Her brother stood to her right, while Blake, an older boy with a buzz cut and oily skin, stood to Hannah's left. They were the last three kids remaining in the game. An assortment of other neighbourhood kids of various ages had either been knocked out or decided to quit early, forfeiting their dollar entry and leaving the park in search of swimming pools and air-conditioned basements. Jacob and Ichiro were the only spectators.

"I'm going to take three strides while dribbling," Hannah said, just loud enough for Jacob to hear from the cool-but-not-quite-cool-enough shade of the elm, "jump, layup, spin around in the air and land facing you two losers."

"Good luck with that," Blake said, a pinch of sarcasm peppering his tone. "I have no doubt you'll make the basket."

"Thank you," Hannah replied nonchalantly. Then, without further pause, she took three strides while dribbling, jumped, did a layup, spun around in the air and landed facing her two opponents, who did happen to be losing. The ball bounced off the backboard and swished through the net. Hannah laughed and dribbled the ball back to Blake. She passed it to him and said, "Thanks again, buddy. Your vote of confidence gave me the boost I needed to make the shot."

Blake caught the ball but didn't respond. With sweat coating every bit of his skin and his cheeks flushed bright red, he looked like he might pass out at any moment. Hayden didn't look much better. Hannah, on the other hand, looked like she could continue playing for hours without needing to take a break.

Blake dribbled the ball twice, then paused to wipe his palms on his camouflage-patterned shorts. He eyed the court before him, no doubt planning the shot in his mind.

"Take your time," Hannah said, and Jacob could hear a smile in her every word. "But just a friendly reminder: you're at H-O-R-S. Miss this shot and you're out."

Blake opened his mouth, no doubt searching for an

insult or comeback, but when nothing materialized he pinched his lips together tightly and turned his attention back to the net. After one more stationary dribble, he started across the baking-hot court. He needed four strides to make it to the net — a slight change from Hannah's shot but not enough to disqualify him — jumped, released the ball, spun in the air and landed, miraculously, facing Hannah. For a brief moment he smiled in disbelief, but the ball bounced twice off the rim and back to the ground without falling through the hoop. Instead of picking the ball up and passing it to Hayden, Blake left the ball and walked off the court, his eyes pointed at his feet. As he passed Hannah he held up a hand without bothering to look at her and said, "Whatever." When he entered the shade of the elm tree he practically collapsed on his back without a word. He draped his arm over his eyes.

"Hey, man," Ichiro whispered to Blake. "You dead?"

"Maybe," Blake croaked through chapped lips. "I'm not sure. But if this is heaven, I want my money back."

Jacob handed over his water bottle and Blake drank half the contents in one long pull, then fell silent again. When Jacob turned his attention back to the game, he saw Hayden land under the backboard, facing his sister, as the ball passed through the net.

"Impressive, baby brother," Hannah said.

Hayden passed the ball to his sister. "You're eight minutes older than me."

"And look how much I've made those eight minutes count."

"Younger, older . . ." Hayden shrugged. "I can beat you."

Hannah gave him a thumbs-up and said, "Okay."

"You're not unbeatable. Do I need to remind you that you have an H?"

"And you're at H-O. What's your point?"

"My point is," Hayden said, his voice rising, "you've missed shots before and you can miss shots again."

"Well, then, by all means, please be my guest and have the next shot." Hannah loved to play the magnanimous sister. It was the most effective way of getting under her brother's skin. As much as she loved him, she also loved to tease him. She passed the ball back to Hayden before he could refuse her offer.

Although he didn't look too thrilled with his sister's slightly less than sincere show of comraderie, he walked to the corner of the court and shot the ball. It hit the outside of the rim and bounced away.

"Aw, too bad," Hannah said. She took a few steps and scooped up the ball. "I thought that was going in."

Ichiro sighed. "I wish they'd hurry up and end this so we can hit the beach already."

The beach sounded good, but the island was where Jacob really wanted to go. It was on his mind nearly constantly, as if it had hooked him on the end of a line and was slowly reeling him in like a fish. He went to bed thinking of Summer's End and woke up dreaming of it. Odd dreams, dark dreams, dreams that thankfully faded away with the morning light. Jacob looked at Blake's inert body. The older boy hadn't moved or made a sound in a few minutes, and he was snoring lightly. Just in case, Jacob whispered. "Instead of the beach, I'd rather go to Summer's End again. There's still so much we haven't seen, and I feel like we're getting closer to the truth of what happened there."

Ichiro's eyes went wide and he looked quickly from Blake to Jacob. Quietly, so low that Jacob could barely make out the words, he said, "Don't let him hear you."

"He's asleep," Jacob whispered. "And even if he was awake, he wouldn't know what Summer's End is anyway."

"I'm not asleep," Blake said, without bothering to sit up or open his eyes, "and I do know what Summer's End is."

Ichiro threw his hands up in the air and glared at Jacob, who felt his spirit plummet. But then the impact of what Blake had said made him take pause. "You know Summer's End?"

"Yeah, I know that cursed house."

"Cursed house?" Ichiro said. "What do you mean by 'cursed'?"

"What do you think I mean?" Blake sat up and eyed them suspiciously. "How many times have you been there?"

"Just twice," Ichiro said quickly, as if he'd been caught doing something he knew he shouldn't be doing.

Blake rubbed his face and ran a hand over his scalp. "Twice, huh? That place has got its teeth in you now, that's for sure."

Jacob laughed nervously. "C'mon, twice is hardly anything."

"That's all it takes."

"What do you know about it?" Jacob asked. He struggled to keep an even tone. "How many times have *you* been?"

Blake scoffed and looked offended. "I've never been," he said. "My brother has."

"Your brother?"

"Yeah, Colin. He's older, left town years ago. He moves around a lot. Anyway, back when he was in high school, he and some friends, they used to go out to that island every weekend during the summer. You know, use it as a place to get away and party. He said there was an old, abandoned house, a huge place called Summer's End.

He and his friends would dare each other to enter but no one was brave enough to take more than a couple steps inside. He loved going but he also kinda dreaded it at the same time. Colin compared the house and his body to a couple of magnets — hold them one way and invisible forces push them apart, but turn one over and they're immediately drawn together."

Push and pull, Jacob thought. *I had the same feeling.*

"Simple," Hannah said to Hayden, her voice cutting through the heat. "Just a granny shot from centre court. You can't miss." She crouched and bowed her legs as if riding the world's smallest invisible horse, then threw the ball underhand from between her legs. It soared high through the air and — *swoosh* — fell straight through the net without touching the hoop at all.

Blake was looking through Hannah, through Hayden, through the basketball and the nets and the trees behind the court. "At first Colin wouldn't stop telling me about those parties. I thought he was trying to show off, make me think he was cooler than he actually was. But the more he went the less he spoke of Summer's End. Until one day his buddy Kent went in, alone. Colin said Kent was inside for less than five minutes but it felt like an hour. When he came out, Colin said Kent was all pale and sweaty. He didn't say anything. He just walked straight to the boats. Wasn't until they were almost home that he turned to my brother and told him what he'd seen."

Jacob and Ichiro sat silent, transfixed, as Blake shared his second-hand knowledge of Summer's End. Hayden cheered loudly, having defied expectations by duplicating Hannah's granny shot. It snapped Jacob out of his trance-like state.

"What did Kent see?" he asked.

Blake laughed, a nervous sound that said *you'll never believe me if I tell you*, but he told them all the same. "Ghosts."

Neither Jacob nor Ichiro said anything for a few moments.

"You don't seem surprised by that," said Blake. "Did you see ghosts there too?

"Nah," Jacob said. "We've just explored the island. We haven't gone into the house yet." The lie came quick and easy. He had no desire to take that particular walk down memory lane with Blake.

"So Kent saw ghosts, eh?" Ichiro said, picking up where Blake had left off.

Blake nodded. "Two of them. And he heard more than that, even." He laughed again, but this time he sounded skeptical and perhaps, Jacob thought, a little fearful. "That's what my brother said, anyway. I don't know."

"Did he say anything else about the ghosts he saw?" Jacob asked, trying to sound casual.

"Yeah. The first one ran down the hallway at Kent. It was a woman. He thought she was a real person until she tried to grab his arm. Her hand passed right through."

Jacob shivered despite the heat. "What did she want?"

"She just whispered, 'James is coming. My husband, he's after me. He will hurt you. Come with me to the basement. We can hide there. We can be safe there forever.'"

"What happened next?" Ichiro asked.

"Another ghost stepped into the hall. He was a big bearded guy in a white apron and he was carrying a leather case. He yelled, 'Get out!' and then he put his case on a table and unlatched the clasps."

Click! Jacob's imagination provided the sound. *Click!* He felt like all the blood had drained out of his head. "What was in the case?"

"Kent didn't stick around to find out."

"What did he do?"

"What do you think he did? He got out of there. Fast. Made a beeline for the boats. No one questioned his story despite how far-fetched it sounded. They all made a pact never to return to the island. After high school, they all moved away and never came back."

Jacob shook his head. The thought of parting ways with friends so willingly was foreign to him.

"My brother never spoke about Summer's End again," Blake said. "Not a single word. I'm telling you guys: that house is cursed." He chewed on his fingernails for a moment of nervous contemplation. "Listen, you can go there all you want. I don't care. But I wouldn't be caught dead on that island."

On the court, Hannah sat cross-legged on the asphalt two metres from the net and tossed the ball through the hoop with one hand.

"Give me a break," Hayden muttered. He grabbed the ball, sat down and yelled in pain. "The court's red hot!" he shouted, and quickly threw the ball. It flew a metre wide of the net, but Hayden didn't seem to care. He jumped to his feet and rubbed the backs of his burning thighs. "How did you manage to sit long enough to get off a decent shot?"

"Guess I'm made of tougher stuff than you," Hannah said. "You're at H-O-R-S, in case you've forgotten."

"Thanks. I haven't forgotten. You keep reminding me."

"You said Kent heard some ghosts," Jacob said, "other than the two he saw, the husband and wife. What did he hear?"

"Oh yeah, right." Blake sighed. The skin on his face, once as red and splotchy as a bloodstain, had turned waxen and white. "He said that was the worst part. The part that nearly drove him crazy and haunted his nightmares for days after he left. When the big man appeared with his case, shortly after the woman tried to lead Kent into the basement, he heard voices from below. Whimpers, then screams.

"They assumed the crying and screams were from the couple's kids. Somebody must have died there, for sure. It adds up, doesn't it? An old, abandoned house on a secluded island, which no one else has moved into for years. An angry husband. A scared wife. And kids hiding in the basement."

Jacob and Ichiro shared a silent look. Jacob's stomach churned, threatening to return the water he had chugged after he had spelled out H-O-R-S-E.

Hayden stood three metres *behind* the basketball net. He shot the ball in a high arc that sailed over the backboard and came close to the rim but missed by a few centimetres.

"And that's E for you, and the game for me," Hannah said. She scooped a pile of change off a tree stump. "And, of course, my winnings." She rattled the change in her fist and smiled. "This takes the sting out of the three-game baseball suspension the league served me. Think I'll spend my newfound free time playing basketball and taking everybody's money."

On a different day, Jacob would have regretted missing the winning shot that Hannah made from behind the net. But after Blake's story, both the game and Hannah's incredible performance seemed inconsequential. They were things that would have mattered a lot more to him before this summer. He felt like his childhood was slipping away.

"And now if you'll excuse me, I'm going to go home, fill my bathtub with ice and sit in it for the rest of the afternoon. I might never get out again." Blake stood to leave, but something crossed his mind and his expression darkened once more. "I almost forgot. Kent told Colin one more thing. As he ran out of Summer's End he looked over his shoulder. The man's apron had a tear in it, as if he'd been stabbed in the heart, and blood was spreading across his chest. The woman's blouse was also soaked with blood, but she hadn't been stabbed in the heart." Blake ran a finger across his midsection. "She'd been disembowelled."

EIGHT

July 31

For more than a week, the dark corners of Jacob's head were filled with horrors every time he closed his eyes. Long hair. Black eyes. Green skin. Claws. Scratching. Tangling. Cutting. Pulling him down, down, down, where he remained with crops of other drowned children forever.

He tried to close his eyes as little as possible. But try as he might to stay awake, sleep always claimed him sooner or later.

As his semi-conscious body slipped through the bed and fell down a long black tunnel, he dreamt of his mother singing him a bedtime song.

Brahms' Lullaby.

Crackle, crackle.

His mother morphed into Tresa. She looked down on Jacob like he was her own son.

"Sleep now," she said. "For when you wake, you will move mountains."

He fell deeper into his dream, farther down the black tunnel.

His mother lay on an operating table. She turned her

head slowly and stared at Jacob with wide, doll-like eyes.

"Don't worry, Jake," she said, void of emotion. "I'll be fine."

Brahms' Lullaby continued to play in his head, although neither his mother nor Tresa sang the words.

"You'll be fine too, Jacob," Tresa said. "Keep falling. Go deeper. We'll be safe in the basement."

Down, down, down he tumbled.

A surgeon with no face approached his mother, blocking her from Jacob's view. He carried an old leather case, which he set down on the operating table.

He opened one latch.

CLICK!

Then the other.

CLICK!

The case opened with a creak that sounded like a rusty scream. Strapped to the inner sides of the case was an assortment of knives and saws. Archaic surgical tools from the 1800s, rusted but still sharp and splattered in blood as bright and red as a cardinal's wing.

The surgeon pulled out a long knife.

Crackle, crackle.

He pulled out an artery hook.

Crackle, crackle.

He pulled out a large surgical saw with a handle.

Crackle, crackle.

The surgeon's facial features slowly appeared. Jacob wasn't surprised to see who it was.

Dr. James Stockwell.

"You shouldn't be here," he said to Jacob, his beard trembling with rage.

And then the doctor turned and went to work on Jacob's mother with his surgical tools, and Jacob couldn't move, and he was forced to watch, and then he found himself on the surgical table in place of his mother, and she stood beside the table, and beside her stood Tresa, and the doctor raised the saw, and Tresa said, "We'll be safe in the basement," and his mother said, "Move mountains, Jake," and Tresa said, "Forever in the basement," and the doctor said, "Time to go," and he lowered the saw, and he sawed, and he sawed, and he sawed . . .

And Jacob stopped falling.

NINE

August 1

Early that morning, long before the sun had risen, Jacob lay wide awake. He watched the tree branches outside the window sway in a breeze that provided little relief from the previous day's pent-up heat.

He'd had another nightmare, but this one was different. This one was worse. Earlier in the week, he'd dreamt of the Kalapik. Last night, he'd dreamt of James and Tresa, of his mother, of himself, and of a surgical saw . . .

He didn't want to think of it. He needed to be with his friends. He wanted to get away. And for some crazy reason, he wanted to go to the very place he'd dreamt of.

He sent two short texts to Ichiro.

> wanna go to summers
> end today?

> we can take h&h. let me
> know and I'll call them

He put his phone on silent and set it on his bedside table, then rolled over and tried to get a little more sleep. As much as he didn't want to dream, he was beyond exhausted. And he felt like he'd need to be clear-headed and alert when he returned to the island.

———

Jacob paused paddling the canoe for a moment to stifle a deep yawn.

"You tired, Jacob?" Hayden asked from behind. "That's the third time you've yawned in the past three seconds."

"Yawning three times in three seconds isn't even possible," Hannah said. She was seated behind her brother and steering the canoe as they glided across Passage Lake.

"Well, he's yawned a lot in a short period of time. Happy?"

Hannah shrugged.

"I didn't sleep well last night," Jacob said, downplaying how awful his sleep had been.

They paddled for a while in silence.

"Ichiro," Hayden said, "tell me again why you named this canoe *Scarlet Sails*."

"Because it's red," Ichiro said flatly.

"Uh-huh . . ."

"And it sails."

"Sure," Hayden said. "But technically it doesn't."

"Maybe not, but I like alliteration," Ichiro said.

"Like *skull* and *slap*," Hannah added cheerfully.

"Skull and slap?" Hayden said. "That's random."

"Not really," Hannah said, and slapped her brother gently across the back of his head.

"Ow! Quit it." Hayden put a hand to the back of his head.

"Just trying to knock some sense into you," Hannah said. "Literally."

"Yeah, well, literally quit it." Hayden turned his back on his sister and started paddling again. "How much farther is this place?" he asked Jacob and Ichiro. "I'm ready to get out of *Scarlet Sails*." He said the canoe's name with a posh British accent.

"Not much farther," Jacob said. "You'll know the island when you see it."

"How?"

Jacob shook his head, knowing what he was about to say wouldn't sound believable until Hayden had seen the island for himself. "It'll call to you."

"Call to me? Like, on my cellphone? I just checked and the reception's terrible out here." Hayden laughed. He was the only one.

Jacob didn't respond.

"And there's a house on the island," Hannah said, going over the few facts Jacob and Ichiro had shared.

"Summer something."

"Summer's End," Ichiro said.

"And you think it's haunted by a psycho doctor and the wife and kids he killed a long time ago."

Ichiro and Jacob shared a sideways glance and then nodded.

"It's not too late to turn back," Jacob said.

"Are you kidding me?" Hannah said. "It sounds awesome!"

"I didn't think you believed in ghosts," Hayden said.

"I don't, and I'm sure these two scaredy cats," she pointed at Jacob and Ichiro, "have allowed their imaginations to get the better of them. But still . . . an abandoned house on an island, filled with weird stuff to explore? And no father—" She shook her head as if she'd misspoken. "No *adults* anywhere in sight to tell us *don't do this* and *don't do that*? Sounds like paradise."

Jacob held his tongue. He had felt the exact same way when he and Ichiro first discovered the island. Now he was beginning to wish they had never found it. But he was powerless to stay away, as if he were on a set of tracks that kept leading him back to Summer's End. He was, he realized, past the point of no return, and the helpless feeling of being out of control terrified him almost as much as the ghost of Dr. Stockwell.

"It's just up ahead," Ichiro said. Jacob heard a quiet

note of fear in his friend's voice. "Through that marsh."

They passed the final few cottages that lined the shore and paddled into the marsh in silence.

The air around them replied with more silence. Jacob and Ichiro were accustomed to the odd stillness of Sepequoi Lake, but Hayden and Hannah both seemed confused.

"What is that?" Hannah said.

"You feel it too?" Hayden asked. "My ears feel like they're about to pop."

"Happens every time," Ichiro said. "You get used to it."

"There must be, like, some sort of magnetic field around here or something," Hannah said. "Think some weird kind of rock in those cliffs across the lake is causing it?"

"Maybe," Jacob said. *Or maybe*, he thought, *it's the island*. But he kept that to himself. The twins, he knew, would come to their own conclusion about the truth. All in good time.

Slap!

"Ow!" Hayden said, throwing his paddle into the bottom of the canoe. He spun around and scowled at his sister. "You slapped me again. What was that for?"

"That was for humming. It was creeping me out."

"I wasn't humming!"

"Jacob? Was it you?" Hannah asked, with a mix of

skepticism and confusion. "Or Ichiro?"

"No," they said in unison.

"I swear I heard someone humming, and when I find out which one of you is lying to me—"

"It was the island's song," Jacob said.

"The what?"

"Let me guess: Did it sound like a lullaby?"

Hannah took a deep breath and nodded.

"It's called Brahms' Lullaby, and I hear it too," Jacob said. "Every time I come here. I hear it in the water. I hear it in the wind. I hear it in my very own heartbeat as if it's infecting the blood in my veins. It's like a disease, but . . . but I'm drawn to it." He shook his head and looked up from the water, then behind. The twins were both staring at him with wide eyes and open mouths.

Hayden half-turned to his sister. "Yeah, he was totally the one humming. Next time, hit him first, not me."

"It wasn't him," Ichiro said. "He's telling the truth. It even played all on its own from an old record player in the house the second time we came out here."

"Do you want to turn back, bro?" Hannah said.

"Nah. You?"

"Not at all."

Jacob turned back around to face the bow and resumed paddling toward the island.

You will, he thought.

As they walked along the overgrown path from the rickety dock to the house, ducking under branches and weaving around nettle bushes, Jacob could have sworn he heard something odd every now and again — a fifth set of footsteps, sometimes trailing them, sometimes to the left or the right, sometimes straight ahead. And just before they left the woods and entered the clearing where Summer's End sat in wait for them, the sound of the footsteps pounded in his head.

He decided not to tell the others.

Not only did it seem far-fetched, but he was also afraid — and not entirely surprised — that the pattern of the footsteps had matched the beat of Brahms' Lullaby.

———

"I stand corrected," Hannah said. They stood inside the front foyer, taking in all of the dust and decay. "This place isn't paradise. It's heaven."

Hayden nodded agreement. "Totally cool. You should've brought us here sooner. I bet this house has a hundred secrets, and now we only have half a summer to discover them."

"We can come back after school starts," Hannah said. "Well, until the lake freezes over."

"Not even," Hayden said. "Ichiro's parents are selling the canoe at the end of summer, remember?"

"It's too bad," Ichiro said. "Blake told us his older brother and all his friends used to hang out on the island when they were in high school."

"He also told us that it freaked them out and they all moved out of town the first chance they got," Jacob said.

"Good point," Ichiro said. "So you're all actually lucky I'm moving away."

"Should we be here at all?" Hayden asked. "If the house freaked out a bunch of teens and the island split up a group of friends, shouldn't we leave, like, now?"

"As long as we stick together, we'll be fine," Jacob said. "Ichiro and I have been here a couple of times and nothing has hurt us. Besides, if anything happens we can always get out and head straight back home."

Hayden nodded, but he still didn't look comfortable with the idea.

"You're all talking like this place is actually haunted or cursed or something," Hannah said. She eyed Jacob and Ichiro. "Did either of you two actually see a ghost when you came here?"

"Blake said his brother's friend saw the doctor and his wife," Ichiro said.

"I asked if either of you saw a ghost, not if either of

you had heard a third-hand account about something that happened years ago from an unreliable source about a kid none of us have ever met."

Relatively certain what Hannah's response would be, but with nothing else to say, Jacob said, "And we heard running feet, laughter and screams."

"Precisely!" Hannah exclaimed triumphantly, actually raising her finger in the air like an overly exuberant prosecutor proving a point. "You *heard*. You didn't *see* anything. It's an old building. It creaks and groans. It's probably full of animals — raccoons and possums and rats."

"Rats?" Hayden said quietly, casting a nervous glance at the floor and shifting his weight from foot to foot.

"Yeah, rats. The footsteps you heard were probably just a bunch of rats scurrying through the house."

"And the laughter?" Jacob asked. "The screams?"

"The laughter could have been chittering squirrels. And have you ever heard raccoons fighting? They shriek like a couple of people who are killing each other."

Jacob knew what he heard hadn't been animals, but he wouldn't be able to convince Hannah. Moreover, he didn't want to fight about it. All he wanted to do was explore a little deeper and hopefully find some more clues about what happened to the Stockwells.

"Fine. It's possible we were mistaken."

"Of course it's possible," Hannah said. She took a few steps down the hall, then turned back to face them. "And once we've spent a few uneventful hours here you'll—"

Hannah paused. She cocked her head, looked under the front-hall table, then bent to the floor.

"What is it, Hannah?" Hayden asked. The four words tumbled out of his mouth in one uninterrupted sound.

She picked something up and examined it in the dim light. It glittered faintly. "It's a necklace."

Jacob looked a little closer. It was the necklace with the pendant in the shape of the letter C, the one they had found taped to the back of the picture frame on the front-hall table the first time they'd been there.

"If you three guys don't mind, I think I'll keep it." Hannah slipped the chain over her head and tucked the pendant under her shirt.

Jacob didn't think that was wise, but he knew Hannah didn't have anything nice like that of her own. He didn't respond, nor did the other two boys.

"So, have you already explored the entire house?" Hannah asked.

"No, just the main floor," Ichiro said. "We looked down the stairs, but I'm in no rush to go all the way down there. We haven't been upstairs at all yet."

"Well, what are we waiting for? Let's check out the

second floor." Without waiting to gain approval from the others, Hannah walked down the hall and up the stairs. Hayden and Ichiro followed.

Jacob couldn't resist peeking into the doctor's office and nursery on his right, and through the adjoining room with the cots. The basement door at the back of the room was still open a crack. He quickly looked away and hurried to catch up with the others.

The wooden steps creaked loudly as he made his way up the stairs. Jacob found Ichiro and Hayden moving slowly along the hallway, tentatively peering into bedrooms but not entering them. Hannah was walking around like she owned the place, entering rooms and exiting them moments later.

"The bedrooms are full of antique furniture," Hannah said in disbelief. "I feel like we've entered some sort of portal and gone back a hundred years. It's bizarre."

Hayden took a step into the nearest bedroom, looked left to right, then stepped back into the hall. "Why is the furniture still here? If it weren't for the way the house looks from the outside, I'd think someone still lives here."

"Someone probably still owns the house," Jacob said.

"Then why wouldn't they live here?" Hayden said. "Or sell the property? I bet this island's worth a fortune."

Jacob could only shrug.

"Are you guys going to stand around in the hall talking all day?" Hannah said, as she walked out of one bedroom and into another without slowing.

It was enough to get the three boys moving. No one wanted to appear scared. Their paths criss-crossed as they went from room to room, pausing to open dresser drawers and closets, and peer under furniture for anything that might be hidden or forgotten. Most of the furniture was made of dark wood and was adorned with intricate carvings and designs. Beds, nightstands, tables and chairs filled each room. It was like walking through an old house that had been turned into a museum.

After swarming through the second floor like insects in search of food, the four friends congregated in the master bedroom at the far end of the hallway.

"Did anyone find anything interesting?" Jacob asked.

The other three shook their heads.

"Me neither."

"I take it no one bumped into any ghosts, either, right?" Hannah asked, with a cocky smile. "Or bumped *through* any ghosts, I guess I should say."

"No, Hannah, we didn't see any ghosts." *But we didn't see any animals either*, Jacob thought.

"Hey, look at that," Ichiro said. He crossed the room

and lifted an ornate frame off a nightstand.

"What is it?" Hannah asked.

"An empty picture frame." It was small and square.

"What's so special about that?" said Hayden.

"There was another one downstairs on the hall table that was empty too. We found the picture that had been ripped out of it hidden in a drawer in the dining room. It was from James and Tresa's wedding day."

"Maybe this frame has always been empty," Hannah said.

"Maybe," Ichiro said. "But I doubt it. Who would keep an empty frame beside their bed?"

"Come to think of it," Jacob said, "I haven't seen a single photograph on display in the entire house."

"Maybe they were too busy framing words and quotes," Hannah said. She pointed at a frame mounted on the wall above a large wooden wardrobe.

A mother's love for her child is like nothing else in the world.

"They're all over the house," Ichiro said. "They give me the creeps."

Hannah unlatched the wardrobe's large doors. They squealed open slowly.

"Jackpot!" she said.

Inside were a dozen or so women's outfits dangling from metal hangers. Hannah pulled one out. It was black, long and sleek and seemed to have been spun out of silk thread that sparkled in the room's dusty light.

Hannah held it up to her shoulders. The bottom of the dress touched the floor. "This is beautiful. Too bad it's not my size."

"Yeah, you could've worn it with your new necklace," Hayden said.

"The necklace I can conceal. There's no way I could keep this from Dad."

"I wouldn't have guessed that dress is your style," Jacob said.

"Just because I don't have anything similar to it doesn't mean I wouldn't like to." Hannah pulled out more outfits, each one from a bygone era and clearly expensive, the type of dresses women wore to balls and gala events. In the bottom drawers there were also hats, shoes and purses to match the clothing. Hannah got to the end of the outfits and examined the final one.

"One of these things doesn't belong," she said with a singsong voice.

It was a long white gown, covered by a white apron. A small white hat fell out of the ensemble and landed on the floor at Hannah's feet. The only splash of colour was the red cross on an armband stitched on to the left sleeve. "It's an old nurse's uniform," she said. She tossed it onto the bed and turned back to the wardrobe. "I like the expensive dresses better."

Jacob looked at the nurse's outfit for a moment and then walked toward it. He felt drawn to it, almost the same way he felt drawn to the island. He ran his hand over the armband, the thin ridges of thread gently scraping over his fingertips like the stitching of a baseball. When his fingers alighted on the cross, he saw a flash of a cardinal's wing followed by a red ball cap, and then the cross was just a cross again. He shivered and quickly withdrew his hand.

"What is it?" Ichiro asked, suddenly at his side.

Jacob hadn't noticed or heard his friend approach. He shook his head. "Nothing. Do you think James and Tresa worked together?"

"Maybe, but who knows if this was even hers?" Ichiro's voice softened as the sentence drew to a close. He noticed something sticking out from under one of the bed's pillows and pulled it free.

It was a square black-and-white photograph of Tresa. She was wearing the nurse's outfit. The image was a little blurry, but she was standing in the middle of what appeared to be a hospital room. Against the walls on her left and right were a dozen cots, each one occupied by children of different ages.

Ichiro turned the photograph over and revealed handwriting on the back. It simply read,

Tresa Stockwell
& Tuberculosis Patients
1915

"I guess now we know the nurse's outfit was Tresa's," Ichiro said. He turned the picture back over and examined it again. "This picture would've fit the square frame on the nightstand, but that doesn't answer why someone hid it."

Jacob looked from the uniform to the dresses on the bed to the now-empty wardrobe. He noticed something odd. It was easy to miss, but there was a small panel of wood in the back, at the bottom, that looked slightly out of place. Upon closer investigation, Jacob realized what had caught his eye. The wood grain of the wardrobe was vertical, while the wood grain in the area he'd noticed was horizontal. "Speaking of hidden things . . ." he said, as he knocked on the panel. It sounded hollow. He punched the wood and the small square popped loose.

"Cool!" Hannah and Hayden said in unison.

Jacob reached into the small secret compartment and pulled out a handful of ripped paper.

"Whoa, what's that?" Ichiro said, forgetting about the photograph of Tresa.

Jacob spread the paper out on the bed and examined the pieces more closely. "It's an envelope," he said, picking up a corner piece and pulling a smaller piece of paper out of it. "And there's a torn-up letter inside." He unfolded the jagged slip of paper and read the cursive handwriting on it.

12 August 1915
Dear Albruna,

Ichiro peered over Jacob's shoulder. "Who's Albruna?"

Jacob shrugged. "I don't know, but this was written the same year that photograph was taken," said Jacob, he put the pieces of paper in his pocket. "We can assemble the pieces like a jigsaw puzzle and tape them together back home, then try to figure out what it says."

After agreeing, Hannah and Hayden turned their attention back to all the clothes they had pulled out of the wardrobe. Ichiro examined the photograph a little further. Jacob found himself drawn to the nurse's apron again.

He picked it up and reached into the pocket without thinking. His hand touched something wet and slimy.

Jacob pulled his hand out of the pocket and held it up to his face. His eyes went wide and his breath latched in his throat.

His hand was coated in blood.

Thick red rivulets ran down his fingers and pooled in his palm. It stank of wet copper and death. Jacob's skin crawled as he stood paralyzed and repulsed.

"What's the matter, Jake?"

Ichiro had spoken, but he sounded far away.

Jacob couldn't think what to say. He looked back at his hand, only now . . .

It was clean.

There was no trace of blood, wet or dry, anywhere on his skin.

Ichiro's face was tight with concern. "I said, what's the matter?"

"It's nothing," Jacob said. He laughed, hoping he didn't sound nervous. "I'm just . . ." He swallowed dryly. "I'm just not feeling all that great. I think I need some fresh air."

"Do you want me to come with you?"

"No, no, that's all right. Stay with Hannah and Hayden and come out whenever they're done doing . . . whatever it is they're doing."

They were trying on hats and shoes from the wardrobe and prancing around the room as if it was their own personal catwalk, pausing only to laugh at each other's ensembles.

"You sure?" Ichiro asked.

Jacob nodded and left the room before Ichiro could say anything else.

———

The sun was at its high point in the sky, weighing down on the world with the full force of its oppressive heat. There was very little shade in the clearing and Jacob didn't want to remain on the covered front porch, so he walked a few paces into the woods and sat heavily against a thick maple tree. He stared at his clean hand.

He couldn't wrap his head around it. He was certain it had been covered in blood. And furthermore, he'd felt the blood before he'd even pulled his hand out of the pocket. Seeing things was bad enough, but how could he explain *feeling* things?

He shook his head and closed his eyes. The image of the apron appeared in his mind. The pocket, Jacob realized, would have rested against Tresa's abdomen. He pictured Blake drawing a finger across his belly.

"*She'd been disembowelled,*" Blake had said. Dr. Stockwell had slit his wife open when he killed her. It made sense — in a twisted, bizarre sort of way — that Jacob would reach into her pocket and pull his hand out covered in blood.

But if that makes sense, Jacob thought, *nothing in the world makes sense anymore.*

When he opened his eyes again, he saw another flash of blood that disappeared quickly.

For a horrifying second he feared the blood was on his hand again, but then he realized it had been farther away, deeper in the woods — out of reach and now out of sight.

Jacob got to his feet. He walked slowly, watching his step, winding around trees, moving closer to the spot where he had seen the blood. It had moved from right to left before disappearing behind a pine tree. Maybe he had caught a glimpse of a wounded animal, like a deer, moving through the forest.

And what would I do if it is a dying deer? he thought. *Would I put it out of its misery, or call Hannah to do it for me?*

As he inched forward he started to believe, started to hope, that he hadn't actually seen anything. He was tired and stressed, his nerves wound up as tight as fishing line around a reel. It was far more plausible that he had imagined both the blood on his hand and in the woods.

The same flash of movement he'd seen before stopped Jacob dead in his tracks.

It was red, but it wasn't blood. It was a hat. A lucky red hat.

Colton.

The boy looked at Jacob with wide, pleading eyes.

"Jacob?" he said in a raspy voice. It sounded like he hadn't spoken in years.

Jacob didn't know how to respond. Even if he could think of something to say, his brain no longer seemed to be connected to the rest of his body. He couldn't move, couldn't speak, couldn't even breathe.

Colton took a step toward Jacob. He walked over dry pine needles and crunchy leaves without making a sound. He reached out a hand. "Help me, Jacob. Please." His final word came out in a wet gurgle.

"Colton?" a man's voice bellowed from the front porch of the house. "What are you doing out here? Get inside. Now!"

Jacob turned and stared in disbelief. It was Dr. Stockwell, dressed in an old-fashioned suit and a bloody apron.

"I have to go," Colton whispered urgently. "If I stay out here any longer I'll be punished. Please help me, Jacob."

The boy turned and ran out of the woods. As Jacob watched Colton cross the clearing, he realized with a sickening feeling that the boy hadn't aged a day since he had disappeared four years before. He was still a ten-year-old boy, although not the healthy, happy child he had been the last time Jacob had seen him.

Colton ran around Dr. Stockwell's large body and disappeared inside. The doctor watched him pass and then turned his attention back to Jacob.

"If you return," he said, in a low voice that carried across the clearing, "you will meet the same fate as that boy." He stepped back through the open doorway and was swallowed up by the darkness of his house.

And then, suddenly free of the madness that had held him in place, Jacob dropped to his knees and cried.

A moment later Ichiro came outside, followed by the twins. They spotted Jacob on the forest floor and ran to him. Ichiro crouched beside him.

"Jake? Are you okay?"

"No," Jacob said.

"We heard voices," Hannah said. "Were you talking to someone?"

Jacob nodded. "It didn't sound like chittering squirrels, did it?" he asked.

"No. It didn't."

"Maybe now you'll believe me when I say this house is haunted, although you might not believe this next part. I'm not even sure I do." Jacob looked at his friends and took a breath, knowing what he was about to tell them would make him sound crazy. But he didn't care. He knew what he had seen, even if he was having a hard time believing his own eyes. "It was Colton's ghost. The Kalapik didn't get him. Dr. Stockwell did."

TEN

August 10

Everywhere Jacob looked, down every aisle and around every corner, he saw Dr. Stockwell. When he entered Connor's Grocery with his mother, he thought the cashier was wearing a bloody surgical apron. When he passed a stock boy near the produce, he thought he was stacking knives and saws, not cans and bottles. Even the cereal aisle wasn't safe — Cap'n Crunch's white moustache briefly turned black and grew to a full-blown beard out of the corner of Jacob's eye.

Crackle, crackle.

The voice of Dr. Stockwell whispered in his head, followed by the grisly sounds of a body being skinned alive, hacked to pieces, placed in a weighted bag and thrown into Sepequoi Lake.

As much as he had hated the dreams he'd had earlier in the summer, the black eyes and the green skin and the fingernail claws of the Kalapik had been preferable to the images and sounds of Dr. Stockwell that now filled his mind. Real-life horrors, Jacob now knew all too well, were far scarier than make-believe bogeymen.

Jacob laughed bitterly. A murderous ghost was now part of his real life.

As was Colton, even though he hadn't been a part of Jacob's life since he'd disappeared four years ago. Seeing Colton in the woods, wearing his red hat and pleading for help, had raised more questions than ever. Answers were starting to take shape in Jacob's mind, and he couldn't wait to get together with Ichiro and the twins to discuss them.

"You all right, Jake?" his mother asked, as she placed a few cans of soup in their cart.

"What?" Jacob asked, as he came out of his thoughts. "Oh, yeah. I'm fine."

"You don't look fine. Have you been getting enough sleep?"

"I dunno. I guess."

"A moment ago you laughed even though I hadn't said anything. And you've been really jumpy for a week or two." She stopped pushing the cart and squeezed his shoulder. "If there's something bothering you, you can tell me."

"I'm good."

His mother frowned and looked at him skeptically, but the hint of a smile tugged at the corners of her mouth.

"I am! Really!" Jacob laughed at the goofy look on his

mother's face. "It's been an awesome summer. I guess I just don't want it to end." It wasn't the full truth, but it wasn't a lie, either.

"You've still got a few weeks left to raise a little hell. No need to get all mopey just yet. Save that for the last week of August, okay?"

"Sure thing, Mom." He smiled.

"You look better already!"

"I *feel* a little better."

"Well, while I'm on a roll toward winning Mom of the Year, tell me something good."

"What do you mean?"

"I like good things, especially when they involve you. So tell me something good. How's your baseball team doing?"

"Not bad," Jacob said. "We lost three games during Hannah's suspension but we're still in second place."

"That's good." She paused for a moment. "You get along pretty well with Hannah. Are you two, um . . ."

"No," Jacob said, trying not to shout. "Absolutely not, Mom. Gross." He looked down both ends of the aisle. Luckily they were alone. Hopefully no one had heard any part of that.

His mother blushed and shrugged. "It's just—"

"She's just a friend. I've known her practically my whole life. She's *just* a friend," he repeated.

"All right, all right. Excuse me for asking." Jacob's mother pushed the cart toward the freezer section. "You know, I saw her with Hayden and their dad here in the grocery store shortly after she was suspended. They didn't see me."

Jacob slowed his pace. He didn't ask, but he wondered where his mother was going with this slight shift in the conversation.

"Their father was . . ." She trailed off and ran her tongue over her lips as if her mouth had suddenly gone dry. "Not happy."

"Hannah was only sticking up for Hayden," Jacob said defensively, as if the twins' father had popped up beside them and Jacob was speaking directly to him. "Sebastien was charging at him. He could've really hurt him if Hannah hadn't stopped him."

"He wasn't angry at her. He was angry at Hayden."

"What? What for?"

"For not fighting that boy." Jacob's mother shook her head. "For 'needing' his sister to stick up for him."

Jacob fell silent. He shouldn't have been surprised. Of course the twins' father wouldn't be upset at Hannah for getting suspended, but instead at Hayden for not standing up to Sebastien himself.

"It's not fair."

The words had escaped Jacob's mouth before he had

even realized the thought had entered his mind.

"What's that?"

He tried to think of a way out of answering, but nothing came to mind. "Sometimes I wish my dad hadn't left, while Hayden and Hannah go through life wishing their father would go away."

His mother sighed. "This is a horrible question, Jake, and I wish I didn't have to ask it, but . . . does he ever hurt them?"

"I don't think so," Jacob said quietly. "Not physically. Just verbally, you know?"

"I know," his mother said sympathetically. "You're right, it's not fair. You don't get to choose your family. But you do get to choose your friends. So be there for them, listen to them and let me know if it starts to get worse. Okay?"

"Okay."

They walked past frozen pizzas, frozen waffles and frozen peas.

"Well, that was an epic fail," his mother said while eyeing the frosted glass of the freezer doors.

"Hmm?"

"Asking you to tell me something good — didn't exactly pan out the way I had intended."

Jacob laughed. "No kidding."

"What can I say?" She shrugged and shot him a smile.

"Sometimes I forget how tough it is to be a teenager. How about this? How about I tell *you* something good?"

Jacob nodded. "Sounds good."

"Well, Bernadette — the daytime server at The Hot Plate? Older than the devil and moves as slow as molasses? She finally decided to retire at the end of the month. Guess who got her shift?"

Before Jacob could answer, his mother shouted, "Me!"

"Congratulations, Mom," Jacob said, as he gave her a hug.

"Thanks, sweetie. Not only is it a little extra pay, but it's Monday to Friday, six thirty to two thirty. I might have to pick up an extra shift here and there to cover for the other servers, but for the most part I won't have to work nights and weekends. We can finally do all that cool stuff we've wanted to do together for years!"

"What cool stuff?"

"I have no idea! But we'll think of something." Jacob's mother laughed and absent-mindedly tossed a bag of frozen mangos in the cart even though neither of them liked mangos, frozen or unfrozen.

"Mom, you're scaring me." Jacob returned the frozen mangos to the freezer and smiled. "But it's great to see you so happy."

"Yes, yes, but I want you to be just as happy as I am and enjoy the rest of the summer. Just check in every now and again and let me know if you're going to be home late, okay?"

"Thank you, Mom."

"And do me a favour and don't get into trouble. And if you get into trouble, don't get caught."

"Deal."

"Well, enough about all that," Jacob's mother said. "Let's go pay and get out of here. I'm making your favourite dinner tonight, spaghetti and meatballs. You'll need your strength for your baseball game this evening. Which reminds me, I need to get spaghetti . . . and meatballs . . ."

———

The smell of grilled hot dogs and fresh popcorn wafted from the food truck that was parked beside the baseball field's bleachers. A few young children watched the game with their parents and cheered on their older siblings, while others chased each other in the park nearby and skipped and laughed and picked dandelions.

The sun sat low in the sky and cast an orange blanket over the horizon. Insects buzzed and chirped and thrummed around the diamond.

The second baseman crept closer to the bag, slowly, quietly.

Even though Jacob had taken a large lead from the

base and the approaching second baseman was behind him, Jacob knew he was there. His senses were heightened, alive with the thrill and the rush of the game. He smelled the grilling dogs, heard the insects' buzz and saw the tension on Hannah's and the rest of their teammates' faces as they sat on the bench. From the bleachers, Hayden clapped and whistled. Standing at the plate, Ichiro tightened his grip on the baseball bat and took a gentle practice swing. The world practically sizzled and pulsed with electricity and nerves. It was the bottom of the ninth. They were down by one with one out. Jacob inched a little farther from second base, his eye on third.

Suddenly, Jacob's focus was shattered by a feeling of pressure that filled his head. He groaned and jogged somewhat blindly back to second base, just to be safe. The moment he stepped on the bag, he heard a woman singing in German. Not near his ears, but directly *inside* them.

Guten Abend, gute Nacht,
mit Rosen bedacht,
mit Näglein besteckt,
schlupf' unter die Deck!

The voice faded away on the final lyric, and the sounds of the game slowly returned as the pressure in his head dissipated. He looked around. Everything was a little blurry. He rubbed his eyes, then noticed Ichiro. He appeared to have called a timeout and stepped out of the batter's box which, Jacob thought, was fortunate timing. Jacob looked at the bench to see if anyone had noticed whatever had just happened to him, but all his teammates were focused on Ichiro. All of them, except for Hannah. She was hunched over with her head between her knees as if she was sick to her stomach. Over in the bleachers, Hayden looked like he was going to throw up.

"You feeling okay, Ichiro?" their coach called out from the bench.

"Yeah, I just . . . Yeah." Ichiro shook his head, knocked some dirt out of his cleats and stepped back into the batter's box.

What the heck was that? Jacob wondered.

His own mind answered. *You know what that was. That was Tresa. Singing Brahms' Lullaby in German. And Ichiro, Hannah and Hayden heard it too.*

Jacob clapped his hands — as much to clear his head as to encourage Ichiro — and took another lead that was considerably smaller than before.

The pitcher took the mound, faced home plate, dropped his hands and tensed. For a panicked split second Jacob thought he was going to spin and try to pick him off. He considered inching back to second base but stopped when the pitcher kicked off the mound and fired a blistering fastball toward home plate.

Ichiro swung hard and fast and connected with the ball on his bat's sweet spot. With a beautiful crack, the ball sailed high and far, deep into centre field.

Jacob jumped back to the base and watched. And waited.

The world around the baseball field grew quiet. Not a deathly quiet; it was a living quiet. A quiet filled with the tense thrums of anxiety and hope. It was a quiet that was ready to explode, regardless what happened next.

With her neck turned to trace the incoming ball over her shoulder, the centre fielder pumped her arms and hustled toward the fence. She reached the outer edge of the field at the same time as the ball. She jumped into the air, kicked a foot against the fence, spun around and reached her gloved hand high above her head.

She caught the ball.

A miraculous catch.

Two outs.

The crowd went wild.

Jacob didn't hesitate. He pushed off second base and barrelled toward third with his head down. One word repeated silently in his brain: *go, go go!*

The third-base coach waved him home. Jacob rounded the base. The only sounds he now heard were the beat of his heart, the rasp of his breath and the crunch of his cleats.

Halfway home he spared a quick glance to his left. The second baseman had caught a throw from the centre fielder. He turned and threw the ball over the pitcher's head.

Jacob ran, his eyes focused solely on home plate, when—

Guten Abend, gute Nacht,
von Englein bewacht,
die zeigen im Traum
dir Christkindleins Baum.
Schlaf nun selig und süß,
schau im Traum's Paradies.

He stumbled and slowed. He slid.

The catcher caught the ball. He tagged Jacob's foot.

The umpire pumped his fist in the air and yelled, "You're out!"

Out. Jacob was out. The Tigers had lost the game.

The crowd went wild again. Some cheered, some groaned, but no one remained quiet. Everyone was on their feet.

Everyone other than Jacob. He remained on the

ground for a while before standing up.

He knew then that Tresa was trying to send him — maybe his friends too — a message. What that message was, Jacob wasn't yet sure.

ELEVEN

August 11

Although the library's air conditioner was working overtime to keep the building cool, the back of Jacob's shirt was still wet from the bike ride there. Through a series of late-night texts after the baseball game the day before, the four friends had agreed to meet there as soon as it opened in the morning. Jacob recommended it as a safe zone, a central location away from the prying eyes of adults.

They sat around the small table in the local history room, removing pieces of paper from the torn-apart envelope Jacob had found in Tresa's wardrobe — *don't think about the bloody nurse's apron*, he willed himself — and fitting them together like a jigsaw puzzle.

"So all three of you heard Colton and Dr. Stockwell's voices when I was outside?" Jacob asked. He dreaded their answers, but he had to ask the question all the same. If they had heard the ghosts too, that made them real — *really* real.

Ichiro, Hannah and Hayden looked at each other, then turned to Jacob and nodded.

Jacob sighed. "Thought so. The second time Ichiro

and I went into the house, we heard running feet and laughter. It must've been Colton following us. Maybe he was working up his courage to talk to me."

"I wonder why he only appeared to you and not the rest of us," Hayden said.

"You're talking about it like it was a good thing," Jacob said. "Trust me, it wasn't. You should be counting your lucky stars, not complaining."

"I'm not complaining. It's just weird."

"What isn't weird about that place?" Hannah asked. "I actually now believe in ghosts. That's messed up."

"Why do you think we all heard the lullaby during yesterday's game?" Hayden asked.

"I think . . ." Jacob said. "I think Tresa needs help. I think she's in trouble, even though she's, um, dead." He turned his attention back to the letter and fit the last two pieces together.

They looked over their work for any glaring mistakes. It was a bit of guesswork, thanks to the cursive writing. But the edges of the pieces all seemed to line up and the writing appeared to flow. So he ripped small pieces of tape off a roll he had brought from home and handed them one at a time to Ichiro, who placed them on the letter.

"All right, what now?" Hannah asked.

Ichiro stood and picked up the letter gingerly, as if

he was an archaeologist handling a priceless artifact. "Now we read it. Drumroll, please," Ichiro said.

The twins began drumming on the edge of the computer desk, but Jacob quickly silenced them with a finger to his lips. "We're trying not to draw attention, remember?"

"That was, like, professional-grade shushing," Ichiro said. "I think you just found your calling as a librarian."

"Ha, ha, very funny."

"No, I'm serious. You and Rio could take turns yelling at teenagers and bugging old men."

"Who's Rio?" Hayden asked.

"One of the librarians who works here," Ichiro said.

"Weird name."

"It's not that weird," Jacob said defensively. "And besides, he's a nice guy."

"See?" Ichiro said with a laugh. "You two were destined to work together! You could be Robin to his Batman. Chewie to his Han. Patrick to his SpongeBob. I'll carry on if someone doesn't stop me."

Jacob held his hands up in the air and laughed. "All right, all right. Enough. Read the letter already, will you?"

"Aye, aye, sir." Ichiro began to read:

Dear Albruna,

I write to you in faith that our dear mother is doing well and that the task of looking after her in her old age has not been too great a burden on you. Not a day goes by that I don't miss you, her and father, may God bless his soul.

I wish I could tell you all is well here in Canada, but I am not prone to lying. It is true that my husband and I want for nothing. We are well fed and clothed, and that is a blessing, especially during these trying times with so many sick and dying. Our home, "Summer's End," is big enough for two or three families, but of course that is precisely the problem.

Oh, dear sister, I fear I must tell you about the tragedy that has befallen me, although I do not wish to think upon it. It is a misery from God, and although I try not to question His will, I know not why He has singled me out in such a cruel fashion. You know how desperately I want children of my own to raise and to love, always and forever. And yet it is with great sadness that I report that I am barren and cannot bear a child. Helping the poor children here at home who are ill with tuberculosis has been rewarding, but it's also a double-edged sword. For I know in my heart that it is not wise to grow too attached to my patients, as when their health improves they will leave me, and I will once again be childless and alone.

It is not an accident that I say I am alone. My husband

has thrown himself into his work and largely ignores me. Worse than that, he seems to hold me personally accountable for my body's failings, and he is taking his anger out on the children he treats. He never once raised his voice in all the years I knew him, and now he yells sporadically at everyone around him, and he has taken to drink.

I am afraid, dear sister. I know not what he might do. He is irrational and unravelling at the seams. I know that it is important for a man of medicine to keep his surgical tools clean and in good condition to prevent the spread of infection and disease, and yet he spends all his free time, well past nightfall every evening, sharpening his knives and saws. I pray to God that he does so purely for work, and not with any other hidden evil intent.

I am sorry, so terribly sorry, to write such a bleak letter to you, and I wish I had happier tidings. But I fear that if I did not take the time to write to you now, I might not have another chance to do so.

Please kiss dear mother for me when you read this, and say a little prayer in my name.

Your sister,
Tresa

Ichiro sat back and sighed. "Well, that's pretty much the saddest thing I've ever read."

147

Jacob couldn't have agreed more. So many elements added up to paint a piteous picture. Tresa's call for help that never reached her sister, her grief over not being able to have children of her own, her isolation in Summer's End, her fear of her husband and his descent into madness, her thinly veiled and uncanny prediction that he was about to kill her.

"See?" Jacob said. "She needs help. She needed it back then," he pointed at the letter, "and she still needs it now. I don't know how she did it, but I'm pretty sure she's using that song to call us to the island." Jacob frowned.

"You're wearing your 'thinking face,' Jake," Ichiro pointed out.

"She said she was helping the poor children here at home. She must've meant 'here in my home country of Canada,' since she was writing to Germany." Jacob shook his head. "It's probably nothing."

"Why do you think she tore up the letter?" Hannah asked.

"Maybe she was afraid of her husband finding it," Jacob said. "Or maybe she didn't rip it, but he did."

"Yeah, that makes sense," Ichiro said. "If he found and read this letter, he'd be furious. Maybe that's what sent him over the edge. And if so . . ."

"If so," Jacob said, picking up on the thought that

Ichiro had left hanging, "the murder-suicide would've taken place in the second half of 1915."

Ichiro pulled the picture of Tresa from his pocket and stood it up between two rows of keys on the keyboard. "The same year this picture was taken. She does look pretty miserable, doesn't she? It all fits."

"Are you thinking what I'm thinking?"

"It's worth a shot . . ."

"You two," Hannah said, "are more like twins than we are."

"Thank you," Ichiro said with a laugh.

"Not a compliment. It's freaky."

"What are you talking about? What's worth a shot?" Hayden asked.

"Last time we were here, Rio showed us how to use the microfilm reader," Jacob said. "We knew the year the Stockwells got married, and that's how we were able to find some information about them and Summer's End. We figured there'd be at least one article the year they died — especially if there was a crime involved — but it took forever just to go through 1906 and we had no idea where to start searching for information about either of their deaths. But now, it might be worth trying 1915."

Ichiro pointed at the filing cabinet that held the *Valeton Voice* microfilm reels. "What are the chances Rio didn't lock that?"

"Only one way to find out." Jacob tried the bottom drawer. It opened. "Still unlocked!" He scanned the boxes until he found the two he was looking for: *1915, Jul. to Sept.* and *1915, Oct. to Dec.* He handed the first box to Ichiro, who opened it and wound the film into the reader the same way they had done before.

"Unauthorized usage of irreplaceable library materials," Ichiro said, with a shake of his head. "If Rio ever finds out about this, you can kiss your chances of being his lapdog goodbye."

"Don't make me shush you again."

Ichiro gave Jacob an exaggerated shiver and they laughed together.

Hannah rolled her eyes. "Like I said, you two are freaks."

"All right, let's see what we can find."

Ichiro scrolled through the days, flying past July and the first half of August. He slowed down when he reached the twelfth, just in case, and their excitement levels rose immediately.

"This is really cool," Hayden said. "I feel like Sherlock Holmes or something."

"Watson!" Ichiro shouted. "Jake could be Watson to Rio's Sherlock Holmes!"

Jacob cast a nervous glance over his shoulder. "I'm never going to be allowed back in the building if you keep yelling."

"We wouldn't want that, now, would we?" Ichiro turned back to the reader and continued scrolling. August 13, August 16 . . . "Just so you know," he said, looking at the twins, "this is like looking for a needle in a haystack, so it might take a while before—"

"There!" Hayden said, pointing at the screen. "Right there!"

"Well, that was fast," Ichiro said.

"Holy . . ." Jacob said in awe, as he stared at the screen. Random words jumped out at him from the article: *bloodbath, cut, stabbed, knives, carnage, gore* . . .

BLOODBATH ON SEPEQUOI LAKE

A murder and a suicide was the climax of a week of quarrelling in an island home turned private sanatorium on Sepequoi Lake when Dr. James Stockwell, a well-to-do man, cut his wife, Tresa Stockwell, across her lower abdomen and then stabbed himself in the heart.

The murder weapon, one of the doctor's surgical knives, was found covered with a mix of the couple's blood on the floor between their bodies in the main hallway. The crime was committed early in the morning on Friday of last week and their quarrel was overheard by tuberculosis patients in an adjoining room. Dr. Stockwell turned his home into a small sanatorium for the treatment of consumptives when the hospital in Gravenhurst, where he previously worked, became overcrowded. Many regarded Dr. Stockwell as a local hero for this altruistic gesture, but that reputation will now be tarnished forever.

Mrs. Stockwell assisted him as a nurse in their home, and the couple were well regarded for their efforts in the fight against the tuberculosis epidemic. Their open-air treatments on their secluded island had already cured eight young children, and of the nine patients who were still in the home as of last week, another seven were close to being discharged with a clean bill of health. Three children had died in the home: Danny Fielding, 6, of Gravenhurst; and Sharon Kennedy, 8, and Jeremy Langdon, 12, both of Valeton. They fell to their illness last month.

Garrett Jones, Valeton's Chief of Police, described the crime scene as a bloodbath. Jones said he has never seen such a horrific scene of carnage and gore in his 32 years as a policeman.

One of the young patients reported that he heard Dr. Stockwell yell at his wife, "It's all your fault," during the argument that preceded the crime, and then told her he'd stop her. The argument abruptly ended there. The children remained in their room until they were rescued when a visiting doctor discovered the tragedy later in the afternoon.

The children further reported that Dr. Stockwell had been irritable for the past three weeks or more, often muttering to himself and yelling at them and his wife for no apparent reason.

It is believed that ownership of the Stockwells' house and their possessions will pass to Mrs. Stockwell's sister, Albruna Cannington, and her English husband, William Cannington, who live in Germany. Dr. Stockwell does not have any surviving family.

Jacob's mind raced as his head spun.

"Um, Jake?" Ichiro said. "What was Colton's last name?"

Sitting in the library's local history room with his three best friends staring at him with grim anticipation, Jacob felt like he'd been crushed by a boulder.

"Cannington," he said. "His name was Colton Cannington."

TWELVE

August 18

It only rained once over the course of the following week, but the storm lasted little more than ten minutes and the ground was nearly completely dry by the time the clouds had parted.

As soon as the sun came back out, Jacob hopped on his bike and continued to ride up and down Main Street. He'd done the same for the past few days, but he still hadn't found who he was looking for.

As he biked around town, he passed countless locals and tourists who all seemed to be preoccupied by the weather, although with opposing viewpoints. The locals were upset that their flowers had died and their lawns had the colour and texture of dried hay, while the tourists couldn't believe their good luck in having nothing but clear blue skies and sun for the duration of their getaways.

Jacob brought his bike to a stop in front of a small barbershop. He shielded his eyes with his hand and scanned the street. There were a few other people walking along the sidewalk, but no one he recognized.

"Where are you, Mrs. Cannington?" he muttered under his breath.

Although he had tried to avoid her for years and was dreading the prospect of seeing her now, he knew it was something he had to do. After he and his friends had discovered that she could be connected to Tresa, he decided he'd have to talk to her. Sensing his trepidation, Ichiro and the twins had offered to tag along with him, but Jacob had turned them down. Mrs. Cannington wasn't well, and he wasn't sure she'd speak to him, let alone four kids surrounding her at once. Plus, he had something he needed to say to her — something he'd been putting off saying for the past four years — and he didn't want his friends there when he said it.

"Son, what do you want with that crazy woman?" an old man asked him.

Jacob jumped. He didn't think anyone was that close. The old man who had spoken was standing behind him, leaning against the frame of the barbershop door.

"I don't know what you're talking about," Jacob said, once his breathing had returned to normal.

The old man laughed. "Oh, right. My apologies. I guess you're looking for the Mrs. Cannington who frequents this very street who *isn't* crazy."

Jacob sighed. "How do you know I'm looking for her?"

"You said her name, not even a minute ago."

"So that's how you spend your days? Standing around listening to strangers?" Jacob didn't know the man but his first impression wasn't a good one.

"Son," the old man said with a smile, "I'm a barber. Listening to people is half of what I do."

"Please stop calling me son," Jacob said. He sat back on his bike and prepared to ride away.

"Hang on a second. Maybe I can help you."

"Why would you do that? Why would you help me?"

"I've offended you, and for that I'm sorry. Let me make it up to you."

"What are you offering? A free haircut? Don't worry, I'm good."

"No, I'm not offering you a free haircut. From what I can see poking out from under your helmet, I can tell you've got a beautiful head of hair just the way it is."

The twinkle in the old man's eyes led Jacob to believe he was being sarcastic. He was just about to ride away without hearing him out when the old man spoke again.

"I'm offering to tell you where you can find crazy Mrs. Cannington."

Jacob hesitated. "You know where she is?"

"Well, I can't say I know where she is for certain. She could be anywhere in the world, I suppose. But chances are, if she's not here on this street, she's sitting in the shuttered darkness of her home. And I can tell you where that is."

"All right, then. Where does she live?"

"I'll tell you, but first you have to tell me something."

"And what's that?"

"You have to tell me why you're looking for her."

Jacob gently bit his lips together to stop himself from saying something that he'd regret. He opted, instead, to simply say, "Goodbye."

"Wait. You have to understand, I can't simply tell a stranger where someone lives. That would be . . . un-ethical." Something in the old man's smile made Jacob doubt he truly believed that. He seemed to be playing with Jacob, probably out of boredom. There wasn't a single customer in his barbershop.

Why did I have to stop in front of his door? Jacob wondered.

"Fine," Jacob said. If nothing else, telling the old man would end the conversation, even if it didn't get him any closer to Mrs. Cannington. "I used to go to school with her son."

"Were you friends?"

"Not exactly."

The old man nodded and pursed his lips, considering the information he'd been given. "All right, I

157

believe you. She lives two streets over, on Bloomington Avenue."

"Which house?"

"It's on the south side of the street, near the bend. I don't know the number, but trust me, you'll know which house is hers."

Without bothering to thank the man, Jacob set off, eager to leave his company. But then an afterthought came to him and he stopped. "You know, since you mentioned ethics, you really shouldn't call her crazy. It's not nice. She's been through a lot."

The old man opened his mouth but no words came out. Jacob rode away, revelling in the fact that he'd silenced someone who so clearly valued the sound of his own voice over the feelings of others.

―――

He'd annoyed Jacob, but the old man hadn't lied. Jacob knew precisely which house belonged to Mrs. Cannington.

Jacob had never seen Colton's home before, but he had a hard time imagining it ever looking halfway normal.

It was a two-storey house made of red brick and white plaster. Each of the windows' blinds was drawn tight and the glass desperately needed a good cleaning.

The paint on the window and door frames had nearly peeled off completely, and the wood appeared to be rotting. The lawn was more weeds than grass and had been left to grow waist high. Amazingly, a single red rose bloomed from a bush that appeared to be dead. Jacob stopped, admiring the rose's determination and will to survive.

Jacob chained his bike to a lamppost, took a deep breath and walked to the front door. There was a pile of water-damaged issues of the *Valeton Voice* on the front step. The most recent issues were from three years ago when the paperboy, Jacob assumed, had decided to stop wasting his time by continuing to deliver to the house.

After rehearsing one more time what he'd say if Mrs. Cannington actually answered the door, Jacob rang the doorbell and waited.

The door didn't open. He couldn't hear any sounds from inside. He rang the doorbell again.

I'll try again tomorrow, Jacob thought, slightly relieved. He turned his back on the door—

—and found himself staring at Mrs. Cannington.

She was standing on the sidewalk with a paper grocery bag clutched tightly to her chest and a wild look in her eyes. Her wispy black hair blew in the breeze and obscured her face, but she didn't bother brushing it out of her eyes or tucking it behind her ears. Her purple housecoat was even more faded than when Jacob had seen her last.

"What are you doing here?" she said. "This is private property."

All of Jacob's practised words — every single one — fled from his mind in an instant, and he was rendered mute.

"Who are you?" she asked, while staring intently at the ground, unable to make eye contact. "Tell me!"

Jacob raised his hands in what he hoped appeared to be a calm and reassuring gesture. "Mrs. Cannington, I'm—"

She dropped her bag and took a quick step backwards. Jacob heard glass shatter inside, and three apples tumbled out. She looked straight at Jacob for the first time since he'd turned around and spotted her. "How do you know my name? Are you a doctor?" She raised a bony finger in warning. "If you take another step toward me, I'll scream."

"What? No. My name is Jacob Callaghan. I'm . . . I mean, I *was* . . ." Jacob sighed and lowered his hands. "I knew your son. We were in the same class."

Mrs. Cannington raised a hand to her mouth. A muffled sob escaped through her fingers.

"I'd like to talk to you about him, if that's all right," Jacob said softly. "It'll only take a few minutes, then I'll be on my way. Can I help you pick up your groceries?"

When she didn't answer, Jacob took that as a yes and approached her slowly. He collected the apples and put them in the bag. His finger scraped along a jagged piece of glass and he winced. He removed his hand and saw something red and wet on his skin.

"Did you cut yourself?" Mrs. Cannington asked sympathetically, despite her still evident concern and distrust.

"No," Jacob said with a laugh. "It's just marinara sauce. See?" He wiped his hand on his pants and held it up to her to prove that he was okay.

She nodded once.

"I think I owe you a jar of spaghetti sauce," Jacob said.

Mrs. Cannington seemed completely unconcerned about her food. "You know Colton?" she asked.

"Yes."

"You two are friends?"

Jacob nodded. It wasn't the truth, not exactly, but he didn't think being completely honest so soon would buy him any extra time.

"Are you sure you're not a doctor?"

"I'm fourteen."

Mrs. Cannington looked up and down the street as if she was concerned she'd been trailed home, then nodded once more. "All right. Come inside."

Jacob wasn't surprised to see that the inside of Mrs. Cannington's house was in no better shape than the outside. In fact, it was much worse. Boxes were stacked in perilous towers that looked ready to topple at the slightest movement. Garbage and dirty dishes were piled in the sink and on the kitchen counter. The worst part, however, was the smell. The humid air was thick with a putrid mix of body odour and rotting food. If the house had an air conditioner, Mrs. Cannington hadn't bothered to turn it on despite the heat wave, and not a single window was open, not even a crack.

Jacob cleared a spot on the counter so he could put down the bag, then opened the refrigerator door. Each shelf was crammed with mystery items that bore more resemblance to science experiments than edible food.

Mrs. Cannington sat at the kitchen table and watched him try to figure out where to put her groceries without offering to help. If she was embarrassed about her living conditions, she didn't show it.

Jacob finished making room in the fridge for the food that needed to be kept cool and decided to leave everything else in the bag on the counter. Red tomato sauce had soaked through the bottom of the bag and was spreading across the countertop. *Not that it matters in this house,* he thought.

"Can I sit?" he asked, pointing at a free chair.

Mrs. Cannington nodded and watched him closely as he joined her.

After their rocky introduction, Jacob didn't know how to begin. His gaze wandered around the kitchen and settled on a dusty framed photograph on the wall to his right. It was an enlarged picture of a young Colton sitting on the shoulders of a man Jacob assumed must be his father. Standing beside them was Mrs. Cannington, virtually unrecognizable compared to the broken shell of a woman who sat across the table from him. In the picture, frozen in a happier time, Colton and his parents all had smiles as wide as their cheeks could possibly stretch. Jacob quickly looked away.

Every second that passed was a second longer than Jacob wanted to spend in Mrs. Cannington's house. He decided to throw caution to the wind and dive right in. "I came to see you because I know what happened to Colton."

A flash of hope passed over Mrs. Cannington's face, and she sat up a little straighter. "You do? Is he okay?"

"No," Jacob said flatly. Lying would do no good, and the longer he looked at Mrs. Cannington, the more he began to believe that she knew more than she was letting on. "He died four years ago, Mrs. Cannington. You do know that, don't you?"

Her face fell and she slumped back down in her chair,

deflated and defeated. "No, I don't know that." She covered her eyes as if blocking out the world could stop its harsh realities from being true, at least within the confines of her mind. She struggled to hold back tears and shook her head.

Jacob found a box of tissues and handed her one, which she accepted and held to her nose. "Thank you," she said, surprising him. After a moment, she added, "I don't want that to be true. I don't think I could handle it."

"You already have. For four years . . ."

Mrs. Cannington's face was etched with pain.

A long moment of silence stretched out between them before Mrs. Cannington said, "What happened to my son?"

"This is going to sound—" Jacob barely stopped himself before he said the word crazy, "far-fetched, but I saw his . . ."

"What? Saw his what?"

He knew what he had to say but found it next to impossible to get the word to pass his lips. "His ghost. I know how that sounds, but it's the truth. I saw his ghost." He eyed Mrs. Cannington, trying to decipher what she was thinking. Her expression was stony, revealing nothing. "I understand if you want me to leave."

She looked up, and hard as Jacob found it to believe, she actually looked a little relieved. "No, it's okay," she said. "This might also sound far-fetched, but I believe you. I've seen things, even before all this." She waved her hands in the air, indicating the kitchen, and Jacob had a good feeling he knew what she meant. *Before my son disappeared. Before my husband died. Before my world fell apart.* "Tell me what else you know. Where did you see him?"

Jacob knew what he was about to say was critical. He watched Mrs. Cannington closely to gauge her reaction. "I saw him on an island in Sepequoi Lake, outside a house called Summer's End."

Mrs. Cannington looked down and fidgeted with the tissue Jacob had given her. "And where's that?"

"Mrs. Cannington," Jacob said, careful to keep a soft, neutral tone, "I know you know where that is."

"And how do you know so much for a fourteen-year-old boy?"

Jacob knew she was changing the subject in an attempt to avoid the truth, but at least she hadn't asked him to leave. "I read an old article from the *Valeton Voice* in the library about the couple who used to live there, the Stockwells."

She remained expressionless.

Jacob didn't see any point mentioning the murder-suicide. "The article said the property passed to William and Albruna Cannington."

"A coincidence. There could be other Canningtons in the area."

"I thought of that, so I took a look online. You're the only Cannington listed in Valeton. In fact, you're the only Cannington listed in the entire Muskoka region. So if you weren't related to William and Albruna, that would be one awfully big coincidence, don't you think?"

After a moment spent staring at a point on the wall over Jacob's shoulder, Mrs. Cannington suddenly looked at him with such pain and sorrow that it nearly broke his heart. Years of grief filled every line on her face and her lips trembled as she spoke. "I told them I didn't want that house. I told them it was cursed."

"Told who?"

"My parents-in-law. I wanted them to sell, to get it out of our family, but they refused. They said no one could live there, that it had been passed down through five generations of Canningtons after . . . after what happened there. And I saw." She nodded. "I saw."

"Saw what?"

"That they were right. My mother- and father-in-law had never taken Bill, my husband, when he was a boy — he didn't even know they owned it. On the surface, it looked like the perfect summer retreat for a young boy. His parents knew that, knew the appeal it would hold for Bill, so they kept it a secret. Until he was an adult and they were too old to guard the house any longer. That's when they first told us about Summer's End, the whole bloody history, and that it was being left to us in their will. When I refused to accept and then threatened to sell it to the first buyer possible, they decided it was time to take us out there. To show us exactly why we could never sell it, could never thrust it upon an unsuspecting family.

"And I . . . saw . . . him."

"Dr. Stockwell," Jacob said. "I saw him too."

"Oh, dear God," Mrs. Cannington said with a gasp. "How did Colton find Summer's End? What did that monster do to my son?"

"Had Colton ever been to Summer's End before?"

"No! Never. I wouldn't have allowed it. Bill and I decided it would be safer to keep the island secret until we needed to pass it on to Colton, just as the family had always done. I had to remove all the photographs of the doctor from the frames throughout the house and hide them. I couldn't stand to look at his face — it was like his eyes followed me wherever I went. Then I removed all the photographs of Tresa for good measure. Bill and I went out there twice a year just to make sure no squatters had stumbled upon it and decided to move in, but we never took Colton. So how did he end up there?"

Jacob felt as if his blood was swelling in his veins and threatening to burst through his skin. Like a mosquito with its needle pinched into a child's arm, unable to escape before it explodes in a bloody mess.

This was the moment he had dreaded more than any other. The admission he didn't want his friends to hear. The secret he had held for four long years.

"I have something to tell you," he said quietly. "Something I should have told you long ago."

Mrs. Cannington looked at him with suspicion and curiosity, but not anger or hatred. That gave Jacob a little confidence to continue, but he knew the anger and hate would likely come crashing down on him soon.

"Like I told you," he said, "Colton and I were in the same class in grade four. We weren't exactly friends, but we had a friendly rivalry and used to dare each other to do stuff. I don't know why. Just stupid kid stuff, I guess."

Jacob paused and took a breath. Tears began to well up in his eyes. It was nearly impossible saying this out loud for the first time ever. But he'd already started, and he knew there was no turning back now.

"The day before he . . ." He stopped, then started again. "We were playing tag in the playground. I couldn't catch him and was stuck being 'it' for a long time, so I wanted to get back at him somehow. I said something so, so stupid. I said, 'I hope the Kalapik gets you one day.' I didn't mean it but I couldn't take it back.

"But Colton just laughed and said, 'The Kalapik's not real. I'm not afraid of a dumb story.'

"I said. 'Oh yeah? Then prove it.'"

A tear escaped from Jacob's eye and slid down his cheek.

"That was the last thing I ever said to Colton," Jacob said. "The next day he disappeared. And I'm pretty sure . . . I'm pretty sure it's my fault."

Time slowed down. Ten-year-old Colton smiled out from the picture behind his mother as she sat silent and still, processing what Jacob had just told her. Suddenly she spoke, but what she said was not what Jacob had expected.

"My husband," she said, pointing at the ceiling, "killed himself two floors up, exactly above where we're sitting now. He tried to hold on to life for as long as he could after he lost hope that our son was still alive. But then the burden grew too great for him to bear. He bought a cord of rope, tied a knot in it and climbed the ladder to the attic. He hanged himself." She turned her finger down and tapped it forcefully on the table. "That was his choice. He had been through such grief — far more than any parent should have to suffer — but that was still his choice."

She placed both of her hands flat on the tabletop and her face softened. "If what you're telling me is true — if my son died at Summer's End — then he decided to go there. And I" — she choked on her words and needed to clear her throat before continuing — "I believe you. Whether or not he wanted to prove to you, himself or God knows who else that he wasn't afraid of the Kalapik, boating out to the island was his decision. And you know something? Knowing that now . . . knowing that now gives me a small shred of peace."

She sobbed and shook and Jacob watched awkwardly, thinking she might want to be alone but thinking it would be rude to get up and leave her.

As he watched her cry, he grew concerned. She was paler than she'd been before and beads of sweat had formed on her forehead.

"Mrs. Cannington, are you feeling okay?"

She didn't respond. She didn't look as if she could. Her head and shoulders were hunched over and she began to gasp and wheeze to catch her breath.

"Oh no," Jacob said, as the gravity of what was happening weighed down on him. He pulled out his phone and dialed 9-1-1. "Please send help," he said when the operator answered. "I'm with a woman who is having a stroke or a heart attack or something."

"Hang on," he told Mrs. Cannington, after the operator

had assured him paramedics were on their way. "Help will be here soon. You'll be okay."

A few tense minutes passed. Jacob wished desperately that there was something he could do. Mrs. Cannington was getting worse by the second.

Her face was now beet red and her eyes were bloodshot. She clutched at her chest and nodded. "Please," she whispered. "If you find my son, if his soul is trapped here, promise me you'll help him."

Jacob nodded vigorously. "I promise, but how?"

"There's a black journal . . . in my bedside table upstairs . . . and in the hall . . ." She closed her eyes and moaned. Every word seemed to be causing her extreme pain. "In the hall there's a . . ." She moaned again, louder than before, and doubled over in pain, unable to finish what she had been saying.

There was a knock at the door and two paramedics entered with a stretcher. They asked Mrs. Cannington a series of questions, but she was in too much distress to answer, so Jacob did his best to tell them what had happened. They strapped her to the stretcher and told him he could come with them to the Valeton Hospital.

"Oh, we're not related," Jacob said. "I was just helping her with her groceries."

The paramedics nodded, loaded Mrs. Cannington

into the back of an ambulance and drove away. It happened in a blur.

Jacob went upstairs and found Mrs. Cannington's room. It wasn't as messy as the first floor — as if she'd been hesitant to touch anything since her son had disappeared. Or maybe she slept downstairs on the couch. Regardless, the room gave Jacob the creeps. So he went straight to the night stand, opened the drawer and dug around through a stack of papers, old batteries and other random items. He found a black journal. He flipped through the pages — it was filled with messy handwriting, but he didn't want to stay in the house any longer than necessary. He stuck the journal in his pocket and raced back downstairs.

He looked at the towers of boxes piled to the ceiling that lined the hallway. "In the hall," Mrs. Cannington had said. But she didn't say where he should look, and she didn't say what he should look for. Jacob patted the journal in his pocket. *Maybe this will be enough,* he thought. He cast a final look at the cluttered hallway and stepped outside, filled with grim determination. *It's going to have to be.*

He had made a promise. A promise he intended to keep.

THIRTEEN

August 25

Ever since he had watched the paramedics take her to the hospital, Jacob had spent all his free time poring over the black journal Mrs. Cannington had told him to take. At the top of the first page was the name of the person who had written in it: Albruna Cannington. Tresa's sister.

Jacob had a hard time deciphering long passages of her scribbled handwriting. It was as if Albruna had written in a great hurry or was totally insane. Possibly both.

Definitely insane, Jacob concluded as he had continued to flip through the journal's pages throughout the week. Most of her thoughts didn't make a lot of sense. At least she had written in English, or else he would have had to painstakingly type the whole thing into an online translator. It was all about Summer's End and the ghosts that haunted its halls and rooms, but her thoughts had a habit of rambling. The pain of what had happened was probably too fresh, too raw.

She wrote,

I hear things. I sense things. I see things. I'm not alone.

and,

Is it not enough that the monster took my sister? Why is he allowed to stay?

and,

My sister, my sister, my sister, oh God, how is this so?

The final two pages in the journal had raised Jacob's curiosity more than any other. On the second last page, Albruna wrote about the basement:

The sight of the monster's medical equipment in that dark and dirty dungeon made me physically repulsed. Who knows what he did down there? I never want to find out.

and,

The most curious thing. One of the walls. It shimmers, like a thin layer of oil glistening on hot pavement. So fine and delicate that my eyes almost didn't see it, and when they did, my rational mind didn't believe they had seen anything at all. But it was there.

and,

That's where I first saw Tresa, standing in that shimmer. Not in front of it, mind you, but in it, actually in it. "Come, sister," she said to me. "Step into the Black Sea. It's lovely in here. We can be together. We can live forever."

and finally,

I was in a daze, like a dream. I almost stepped through. But then Tresa's eyes narrowed, her skin grew pale and blood spread across her stomach. I ran. I heard footsteps trail me, but I didn't look back.

On the final page, Albruna had written,

I went back. I couldn't stay away. It was like my sister was calling me somehow. I don't understand it. I went straight to the basement. I stood before the shimmer, what Tresa called the Black Sea. I don't know what I wanted at that moment. To join her in there? To see her one last time before saying goodbye forever? I still don't know.

She came through the wall. I knew she wasn't real but she looked real. How else do I say this? She looked like a real, physical thing in a world of mist and shadow. She beckoned me. I took a step forward. I wasn't thinking. I wasn't in control. She smiled and reached out to me, but then her smile fell. My chest began to burn and I thought I was having a heart attack. It took me a moment to realize it was the chalcedony pendant I wore around my neck. I removed it from under my shirt. It grew hotter in my hand. "You cannot bring that," my sister said. In that moment, her face had changed. She was no longer my sister. She looked different somehow. I took a step backwards, broken free from the trance I had fallen into. I quickly left while my sister yelled at me to return. As much as I wanted to be with my sister, I'm not done with life yet. I haven't been back to Summer's End since.

I don't know how much longer I can resist. Even as I write this I feel the pull.

That was the last thing Albruna had written in the journal, and it had given Jacob plenty to think about. Tresa had been young, beautiful, healthy and rich. She lived in a dream home on her own island and gave back to the community by helping her husband's young patients in their home. And yet, nothing Jacob had learned about her led him to believe she had known much happiness during her short, tragic life. The one thing she wanted more than anything — children of her own — had not been granted to her.

He had a family. It might be small, but Jacob knew that didn't matter. He knew his mother loved him fiercely, and he loved her in return. They might not live in a large house like Ichiro's family, and his mother might need to work at The Hot Plate well into her retirement age, but that didn't matter either. They had each other.

The moon was bright and round in the sky, just a few slivers shy of full. Jacob leaned against the family-room couch and stared at the stars outside. When he was younger he used to spend hours staring at the night sky, wondering what was out there. Was there life on other planets? When did the universe come into existence? How big was it? When would it all end?

He loved those big, unanswerable questions, even from a very young age. They were grand and mysterious. They made him feel small but also part of something bigger, and that gave him comfort. More than anything, staring out into space made him feel lucky that he had his mother, that he wasn't alone in the world. And so, whenever he felt bad that his father was . . . wherever he was, he'd gaze into the celestial heavens and lose himself for an hour or two. When he emerged from his nighttime daydreams he always felt a tiny bit better than he had before.

"You want some dessert, sweetie?" his mother asked, gently rousing Jacob out of his thoughts and bringing him back to the present. He was no longer an eight-year-old boy staring at the stars but a fourteen-year-old thankful for what he had. "Some ice cream, perhaps? I'll crumble some Oreos on top."

His mother's voice sounded distant, as if only a small part of Jacob's soul was on earth while the rest floated amongst the constellations.

"No, thanks. Not really hungry."

His mother crossed the room and sat down on the couch beside Jacob. She touched his forehead and looked deep into his eyes with a twinkle in her own.

"Mom, what are you doing?"

"Checking to see if you're sick. That's one of only two explanations I can think of that would make you turn down ice cream."

Jacob tried to hold back a smile but failed. "I'm not sick."

"Alien abduction, then. What have you done with my son, Pod Person?"

"Mom, stop!" He pushed her playfully and laughed. "Did you know that in Japan they have octopus ice cream?"

Jacob's mother looked up at the ceiling and licked her lips as if magically conjuring the flavour of octopus ice cream. "You know something? That doesn't sound half bad."

"Yes it does! It sounds *full* bad."

"I'd try it," she said with a shrug. "Japan, eh? Did Ichiro tell you about it?"

Jacob nodded.

"You're still upset that he's moving away." It wasn't a question.

Jacob nodded again.

"I understand," his mother said. "Saying goodbye to a friend is never easy. Have you told Ichiro how you feel?"

"A little, I guess."

"He's probably feeling the same as you."

"I know," Jacob said. He thought back to the beginning of summer break. He and Ichiro sat facing each other in *Scarlet Sails*, drifting in the middle of Sepequoi Lake. They'd just discovered Summer's End for the first time and had decided to make the most of their remaining time together. That was seven and a half weeks ago.

And now, the summer was nearly over, like a droplet of water nearly dried up in a drought.

"We promised each other," Jacob said, "back in early July, that we'd make this an epic summer. And it has been. Not in the way we anticipated, but it's been great."

His mother smiled at him sympathetically, as if she could guess the gist of what he meant. But how could she know? She couldn't. No one could.

"I know he's moving and there's no stopping it," Jacob said, "but I still don't like it."

"You don't have to, and that's okay. My parents and

I moved to Ottawa when I was in my last year of high school. Do you think that was my idea? Of course not. And I'm not going to lie: it was pretty terrible leaving all my friends in the middle of the school year. That was hard enough, but when I got to my new school I had a really tough time fitting in. But I got through it on my own, knowing it was only a few months and then I could get out of there and go to college or get a job. None of my classmates would remember me after a few years had passed, and I'd made peace with that. But then, at graduation, as I stood to receive my diploma in front of the entire graduating class, I tripped on my robes and fell off the edge of the stage. I flashed everyone on my way down. I doubt many people forgot me after that. They're probably still talking about it in Ottawa. That's part of the reason I moved back here."

Jacob's mother trailed off as if she had forgotten where she was and who she was talking to. Her cheeks reddened furiously and she gave her son a look that was half apology, half embarrassment.

Jacob couldn't help but laugh. "Great pep talk, Mom."

"I'm not very good at this, am I? I guess what I'm trying to say is I understand what you're going through because I once went through it too."

"I've never flashed anyone."

"You're young, give it time." His mother smiled. "I'm

here for you, Jake. Always have been, always will be."

"Thanks, Mom. I know."

"And," she said, drawing the word out, "my parents were there to see my scandalous show onstage, and I guess they felt really bad for me, so they bought me my silver necklace with the green gemstone. After I sold my wedding ring, it became and still is the only piece of jewellery I own." She shrugged. "So, silver lining." She chuckled. "Silver lining, silver necklace. That's a good one."

She gave him a wink, opened a book and began to read.

Jacob turned back to the quiet stars, beacons of light in a sea of black. They were peaceful, soothing and put his mind at ease.

So many mysteries out there, he thought.

"Mom?" Jacob asked, pulling his gaze away from the stars and back into the closeness of his family room.

His mother looked up from her book. "Yes, Jake?"

"I love you," he said.

They hugged.

"I love you too. Now, how about that ice cream?"

"As long as it's not octopus."

"You're in luck. We're fresh out."

Black clouds rolled across the sky, blotting out the stars.

Jacob tried not to stare at the clock. He had turned off the TV a little after ten o'clock. All the news channels were tracking a big storm the meteorologists expected would hit the Muskoka region sometime during the weekend. On his desk, his neglected ice cream bowl was filled with goopy sludge. Oreo crumbs floated on the surface like a layer of dirt.

Crick-crick-crack.

Jacob flinched and looked at his bedroom window, where the sound had come from. It had sounded like an animal trying to get in, but his bedroom was on the second floor.

Crick-ca-crick-crick-crick.

There it was again.

He slipped out of bed and crossed the room, slowly, and felt a little silly. Why was he hesitating? What did he expect to find outside in his backyard? The Kalapik? Dr. Stockwell?

Hiding behind the wall beside his window, Jacob pinched the curtain and slowly peered around it.

There was someone in the backyard. Hunched over and rummaging through his mother's garden. A dark, shadowy figure hidden in the night.

Jacob wondered if it could be a homeless person

scrounging for something to eat. There weren't many homeless people in Valeton, but who else could it be?

Jacob had nearly decided to wake his mom and call the police when the figure stood and looked straight at him. He felt his heart seize. It was too late to move or hide. Standing in the light of his room, Jacob had definitely been seen.

The figure dropped a small handful of rocks and wiped his hands on his pants, then raised his hand in greeting. Jacob's eyes continued to adjust to the difference in light between his room and the backyard. Details in the figure's face sharpened and came into focus.

It was Ichiro.

Jacob unlocked the window and slid it open. "Ichiro?" He couldn't keep the surprise out of his voice. "Is that you?"

"Hi, Jake."

"What are you doing here?" He turned and looked at the clock. "It's nearly midnight."

"I know. Can we talk?"

"Of course." Jacob quickly glanced over his shoulder in the direction of his mother's room. "Wait there. I'll be down in a minute."

After closing the window, Jacob grabbed the black journal and quietly crept down the stairs. The back door uttered a small, weak creak when he opened it.

Jacob hoped it hadn't been loud enough to wake his mother.

A howl of wind streaked through the backyard as soon as he set foot on the grass.

"What's up?" Jacob asked. "Why are you throwing pebbles at my window in the middle of the night instead of texting me?"

"My mom confiscated my phone."

"Why?"

"Never mind that. I've got to show you something."

"And it couldn't wait until tomorrow?"

"No, it couldn't wait until tomorrow. Can I borrow your phone?"

"Sure." Jacob took it out of his pocket and handed it over.

"Thanks." Ichiro took it and noticed the journal Jacob had brought outside. "What's that?"

"I'll tell you after. You're the one who came to my house in the middle of the night, remember? You can't just build up the suspense like that and then not deliver. Show me what you want to show me."

They sat on an old, unused swing set that had rusted in a back corner of the backyard for years. Flakes of peeling paint clung to the metal frame. Under their weight the swings squeaked and squealed.

"I've been doing some digging the past few days,"

Ichiro said as he typed quickly on Jacob's phone, "and I've found some things."

"All on your own? I'm impressed."

"You're not the only one who can pretend to be Sherlock Holmes. Turns out I'm pretty good at sleuthing too." Ichiro smiled.

Jacob returned the smile and decided not to mention that Sherlock Holmes had solved all his cases without the use of the Internet and a smartphone. "What did you find?"

Ichiro went to the Valeton Public Library's website. "I tried to find newspaper articles about missing kids in Valeton. I thought maybe I'd find some pattern or something. But I couldn't find anything on Google. Nothing! It's like all the newspapers outside of Valeton don't even know this town exists."

"That's weird," Jacob said. "You'd think missing-child cases would show up in other newspapers, especially since there have been so many disappearances over the years."

"And I didn't find anything from the *Valeton Voice* either, even though I could've sworn I remembered there being articles in the paper about Colton." Ichiro smiled again. "Ask me what I thought of next."

Jacob rolled his eyes but gave in to his friend's request. "Whatever did you think of next?"

"Something Rio had said the first time we visited the library. He told us he was working his way back in time, digitizing the *Valeton Voice,* and that he had only made it to 1955 so far."

Jacob laughed, genuinely impressed. "How did you remember that?"

"Back in time? 1955? Hello? McFly? Anybody home? I immediately thought of *Back to the Future,* and how could I *not* remember that? Didn't you?"

Jacob shook his head. "Let it never be said that a life devoted to pop culture is a wasted one."

"So I signed up for a card — Rio got all misty-eyed — and returned home to log into the local history database. Turns out, um, you don't actually need a card to log into the database. But on a side note, did you know you can use your card to borrow video games . . . *for free?*"

"Yeah, of course."

"Why didn't you tell me sooner? I borrowed *Kill Screen* the day I got my card but still haven't figured out how to beat it even though I've been playing it all week. That's kind of why my mom took away my cellphone. No technology for a week."

"Back to the database," Jacob said, eager to get his friend back on track.

"Yes, right, the database. I typed in a few key search

terms, and sure enough, I found articles about missing kids. A whole bunch of missing kids. In fact, I found a case of a missing kid every four years. Starting with Colton and going as far back as the *Valeton Voice* has been digitized." Ichiro handed the phone over to Jacob. He had bookmarked articles in his personal account, and Jacob scrolled through them, reading the headlines.

Local Boy Missing

Valeton Girl Disappears without a Trace

Authorities Unsuccessful in Search for Missing Boy

Mother Blames Daughter's Disappearance on Legend of the "Kalapik"

On and on and on. Jacob felt sick to his stomach and had to stop scrolling.

"It's like the doctor is on a schedule or something," Ichiro said. "Like he needs to kill every four years with surgical precision, if you'll pardon the pun."

"Precisely every four years. That means . . ."

"That he's going to kill again before this summer is over," Ichiro said, finishing Jacob's sentence.

A hollow silence stretched between the boys as they stared at the ground. A gust of wind threatened to push Jacob off his swing. He planted his feet and gripped the chains a little tighter. The metal was cold.

"We have to stop him," Jacob said. *And if I stop Dr. Stockwell, maybe that will set Colton's soul free.*

"How?" Ichiro asked.

"I'm not sure, not yet." Jacob held up the journal. "But I think there's a clue in here that will help. Mrs. Cannington gave it to me."

Jacob's phone *dinged*. Hayden had texted him.

> Dad's in a mood.
> Can we come over?

"It's Hayden," Jacob told Ichiro. "I think they might need somewhere to spend the night." He sent Hayden a quick reply.

> Of course.
> Ichiro's here.
> We're in the
> backyard

The twins arrived in record time, leading Jacob to believe that their father's "mood" was especially bad.

"I think he had a bad day at work," Hayden said. "Came home with a black cloud over his head. Went out to the bar and we didn't want to be there when he returned."

"I'm not going back for the whole weekend," Hannah said. "It's better to let him cool down completely."

"You can stay at my house tonight," Ichiro said. "If we use the basement entrance my parents won't even know you're there until I tell them in the morning. Don't worry, they'll be cool with it."

"Thanks, man," Hayden said. "Will your parents be okay if we stay over two nights?"

"Well, Jake and I already talked about that before you got here."

"We're going to spend tomorrow night at Summer's End," Jacob said. "Camp out on the island. And we were wondering if you want to come too." He told them about his talk with Mrs. Cannington and the journal she had given him, then showed them Ichiro's proof that Dr. Stockwell had killed a child every four years. "We think he's going to kill again by the end of this summer."

"Huh," Hayden said, allowing everything to sink in.

"If that's true, shouldn't we be worried that his next victim will be one of us?"

No one answered.

Hayden continued. "I mean, shouldn't we avoid the island — heck, the entire lake — like the plague?"

"You're right," Jacob said. "If we go to Summer's End, we're putting our lives in danger. But if we don't go, what then? If I sit here and do nothing and some other kid goes missing . . ." He thought of Colton, saw himself telling him he wished the Kalapik would get him on a Thursday afternoon in June, finding his chair empty the following Friday morning. "At least we have a fighting chance. I think we know more about the doctor and the island's history than anyone else in town, including Mrs. Cannington."

"So why don't we take all this information to the cops, let them deal with it?" Hayden said.

"No." Jacob shook his head. "No, that won't do any good. If we show them all the newspaper articles, the photo of Tresa, the letter we pieced together, this journal, what does it all add up to? Nothing, other than something terrible happened at Summer's End a long time ago. And if we tell them we think the house is haunted they'll laugh us out of the station and then order psych tests for each of us."

"Jake's right," Ichiro said. "No one will believe us. If

anyone can put a stop to Dr. Stockwell, it's us."

Jacob sighed and looked at each of his friends in turn. "I have a feeling that if we can somehow force Dr. Stockwell into the Black Sea and, I don't know, seal it up or block the entrance somehow, we can trap him there forever. I get it if you don't want to come, but I'm going." He nodded resolutely. "I'm going."

"What kind of friend would I be if I let you go on your own?" Ichiro said. He gave the twins a sheepish look. "No pressure, guys."

"No pressure?" Hannah laughed. "That's a metric ton of pressure. But even if it wasn't I would've said yes too."

"Well, I'm not going to be the odd man out," Hayden said. "Plus, I'm in no rush to go back home. I'm in."

"Bring some food, whatever gear you want and some money for snacks." Ichiro pointed at the twins. "You can borrow some clothes and backpacks from me. I've got a tent we can use, and of course *Scarlet Sails*."

"Still a dumb name for a canoe," Hayden pointed out dryly.

Ichiro ignored the jibe and carried on outlining his plan. "Jake, I'll tell my parents I'm sleeping over at your house tomorrow night and you can tell your mom you're sleeping at mine. Let's meet at East Road Convenience at three."

"Three in the afternoon?" Jacob said. "Why so late?"

Ichiro shrugged. "I don't get up before noon. Plus, my parents are going out early in the afternoon for some sort of work function, so they won't see us if we leave then. It's a perfect plan."

Jacob had to admit it did sound pretty good, but he couldn't help thinking of one of his mother's favourite expressions: Man plans and God laughs.

With fist bumps and back-slaps they said goodbye. Ichiro, Hannah and Hayden snuck out of the backyard. Jacob lingered outside a little longer.

The sky was a dark blanket that hung above his head. The air was electric, hot and suffocating. But there was also a chill to the night that seemed out of place, like a lone red rose growing in a dead garden. He felt a quiver in his stomach, deep down under everything.

He had a feeling, as certain as he knew his own name, that Valeton's heat wave was about to break.

A storm was coming.

FOURTEEN

August 26

The sky was red.

Water poured down from the heavens above and flooded the land. The oceans and seas and lakes swelled. The world was washed away. All of it, in the blink of an eye, gone.

A woman's voice sang — *crackle, crackle* — in Jacob's head as he awoke to the new world.

Good evening, good night—

He treaded, desperately trying to stay above the surface. He yelled and screamed for help but no one was around to hear him. He turned, but in every direction there was only water, water, water, water. It lapped against his face, burned his eyes, choked his throat. He dropped below.

Down, down, down.

He twisted and twirled and became disoriented. He no longer knew which way was up, which way was down.

The woman in his head continued to sing, as if it was to be the last song sung on earth and nothing — not even the end of the world — was going to stop her from finishing.

With roses covered—

Underwater, a sea-soaked voice: "Don't worry, Jacob. This will all be over soon. Come down with me. Come down where it's safe."

Tresa floated out of the murky depths, through darkness and seaweed and sludge.

With cloves adorned—

"Behind you," she yelled in near silence.

Jacob turned. A metre behind him was a hideous version of Dr. Stockwell, with long hair and green skin and black eyes and long fingernails. He raised a knife.

Slip under the covers—

Jacob yelled and an explosion of bubbles poured out of his mouth. He found the strength to swim, kicking his legs and pulling his arms and madly hoping he was going in the right direction. After a panicked second that became two, three, four, five panicked seconds he burst through the surface and sucked air into his lungs in messy, ragged gasps.

Tomorrow morning, if God wills—

But he knew he was far from safe. The Kalapik was still beneath him. At this very moment, the monster was swimming up to grab him, to claw at him, to scratch him, to cut him, to pull him back down and never let him go.

you will wake once again—

Maybe, Jacob thought, *maybe it would be better to go with Tresa. Safer. A last resort.*

Good evening, good night—

Something floated on the water's surface, sparkling in the blood-red sunlight. A necklace. Jacob reached for it as if it were a life preserver. As soon as his hand grabbed hold of the pendant and chain, he was suddenly standing. Dry. On land.

In the basement of Summer's End.

It was dark. Hard to see. Cold and staid. Silent.

"Good."

Jacob spun around.

Tresa: "You came."

By angels watched—

Clump, clump, clump. The sound of footfalls. Heavy. Coming down the stairs.

"Oh no. My husband. He found us."

Thump, thump, thump. The sound of a heartbeat. Jacob's. Banging against his chest.

Dr. Stockwell: "I told you if you returned you'd meet the same fate as Colton."

Colton: "Jacob!" His voice came from the wall. *Not from it*, Jacob realized. *From within it.* "Help me!"

Who show you in your dream—

Dr. Stockwell: "Now it's too late." He walked slowly down, down, down into the basement and gripped his bloody knife tight, tight, tight in his clawed hand.

Jacob couldn't move, couldn't think, couldn't breathe. The basement grew darker, colder.

Tresa: "Quickly, now! In here. Before he gets you too." She pointed at the wall — the screams and wails of ten or twenty or more children joined Colton's in a frenzied chorus of fear — and held her other hand out to Jacob.

the Christ-child's tree—

He looked from her hand to his own. He held something. He uncurled his fingers. In his palm was the necklace he had grabbed from the water's surface. Its chain was wrapped around his wrist and forearm three times, like a snake.

The necklace began to glow red. It grew hot against his skin.

Dr. Stockwell was right behind Jacob.

Crackle, crackle.

The doctor raised his knife above his head. It was poised to come down, quivering to pierce Jacob's skull.

Sleep now blissfully and sweetly—

Jacob raised his hand to block the blow.

The necklace's chain slithered off his arm.

The pendant burned even brighter and hotter in his palm. Its red light lit up the basement.

Dr. Stockwell's black eyes flicked and suddenly looked human again. Wide, and full of terror.

see the paradise in your dream—

And Jacob knew.

Jacob knew the ghost could be stopped.

Jacob knew Dr. Stockwell could be defeated.

———

Jacob woke.

Tired, weary, more than a little disturbed, but also hopeful. He had a plan, he had his friends and he believed in himself — that's all he needed.

His dream began to slip away like a snake in the grass.

Like a snake . . .

The necklace. It saved me from drowning and it stopped Dr. Stockwell.

Jacob grabbed the black journal before his dream could flee farther away, and flipped to the final page. He scanned Albruna's mad writings and found the passage he was looking for.

My chest began to burn and I thought I was having a heart attack. It took me a moment to realize it was the chalcedony pendant I wore around my neck. I removed it from under my shirt. It grew hotter in my hand.

The similarities between this and his dream were striking. Jacob wondered if that was a simple coincidence, or if reading the journal had influenced his dream, but no, he felt — he *knew* — that this was the key to defeating Dr. Stockwell.

Chalcedony, he wondered. *What's chalcedony?*

He searched the word on his phone and opened a website about gemstones. At the top of the page was a short description.

Chalcedony, named after the ancient Turkish seaport Chalcedon, is a type of silica composed of very fine intergrowths of quartz and moganite. It has been a popular stone used in jewellery design for thousands of years, and has been worn by ancient Greek sailors as protection from drowning and by early Europeans to ward off evil spirits.

There's the proof, Jacob thought. *Definitely not a coincidence.*

There were many different colours and varieties of chalcedony gems pictured on the website, including one green one that looked similar to his mother's necklace.

He got out of bed and crossed his room. His fingers trembled as he pulled the curtain across its track and looked outside. It was as if he'd cut the belly of the sky open and flooded his room with its light. The blood-red sunrise was beautiful and awe inspiring. It was also a little intimidating.

Red sky at night, sailor's delight.

He had hoped the storm would pass, but he knew all too well what the colour of the morning sunrise foretold.

Red sky at morning, sailors take warning.

He got dressed and waited for his mother to head down to the kitchen.

When the coast was clear, he snuck into her room. In the jewellery dish on her bedside table, her necklace glinted in the morning light. He picked it up and warily slipped it into his pocket, half expecting it to slither back out and feeling more than a little guilty about taking it.

I'm just borrowing it. I'll return it.

His phone rang. It was Ichiro. He answered it quickly and slipped back into his room, then closed the door gently.

"Hey, man," Jacob said quietly. "You're up early. You guys have an all right night?"

"Hayden got up three times to pee and Hannah is a champion snorer, so I'm pretty groggy, but otherwise we're peachy. You?"

"Yeah, I slept fine." Jacob didn't feel like reliving the parts of his dream he could still recall quite so soon after waking. "What's up?"

Ichiro paused. "Did you see the sky this morning?"

"Yeah. It was kind of hard to miss."

"Hard to miss? It was blood red." Ichiro paused, then added, "A bad omen."

"Don't worry about it, Ichiro. That's just an old wives' tale."

"Yeah, well, tales sometimes become old wives' tales because there's truth to them."

"Are you trying to say we shouldn't go to Summer's End today? Because as I said before, we don't have any time to lose."

Ichiro sighed. "You're right. Today's the day."

"Rain or shine?"

"Rain or shine."

———

The rest of the morning was, surprisingly, all shine, no rain. The red faded to pink and then mellowed to a soft blue, but in the eastern horizon hung a bulbous black cloud that swelled like a tumour. Jacob tried not to look at the cloud as he packed his overnight gear.

Into his backpack went a pair of jeans and a hoodie sweater in case the night got cold. He slid a few comics in the back, careful not to bend or tear the pages, and on top of everything he placed the journal and Tresa's taped-together letter.

A small coin jar sat on his desk. Jacob opened it and spilled his change on the tabletop. He had $14.35 in dollars, quarters, dimes and nickels. The sum total of his savings. He swiped the coins off the edge of the desk into a sandwich bag.

Last, but certainly not least, he slipped his mother's chain over his head and tucked the pendant behind his shirt. He felt a little silly wearing a piece of women's jewellery, but no one would see it and he hoped it might protect him and his friends.

Jacob looked in the mirror. A frightened teenager with a backpack slung over one shoulder looked back at him. "Snap out of it," he said. "Be brave. It's just one night. There and back again. Possibly the last time the four of us will do something like this together."

One last adventure.

———

When he entered the kitchen in search of breakfast, he found his mother sitting at the table, sipping a mug of coffee and working on another crossword puzzle.

"Lazybones," she said, without looking up.

"Let me guess," Jacob said, looking over her shoulder at the newspaper. "A nine-letter word for an idle person."

"No, it's not from the crossword puzzle this time. I'm

just calling you a lazybones."

"Mom! It's not even ten yet."

"The early *cardinal* gets the worm," his mother said.

"The early cardinal? Why would you say that?"

His mother laughed and looked at her son quizzically. "I didn't. I said 'the early *bird* gets the worm.' Do you need to get your ears checked?"

Jacob tried to cover by laughing with a shrug. "No, my ears are fine. Maybe I need more sleep."

"Well, I can't help you with that, but I can feed you, and that's equally important. There are fresh eggs in the fridge. If you mix them in a bowl, I'll cook us some omelettes. What do you say?"

"Sounds good."

Between mouthfuls of egg and cheese, Jacob said, "Ichiro invited me to sleep over at his house tonight. Is that cool?"

"Yeah, of course that's cool." His mother ran her napkin across her lips and smiled. "What kind of trouble do you two plan on getting into?"

Jacob shrugged and looked at his plate. He hated lying to his mother, but he was committed to the plan. "We'll probably just play some video games and watch a couple of horror movies in his basement."

"Sounds like you're not going to get much sleep."

You have no idea, Jacob thought.

At three o'clock sharp, Jacob coasted down the hill to East Road Convenience. Ichiro was already there but he was alone.

"Where are the twins?" Jacob asked.

"They called home this morning to tell their mom they're staying at my place tonight. She said their dad was out, so they decided to go back quickly to grab some stuff."

Jacob removed his helmet and ran his fingers through his hair. He slipped off his backpack and rested it on the ground. With a sleeping bag tied to its bottom and some food he'd snuck out of the kitchen (half a loaf of bread, a jar of peanut butter, three apples and two bottles of water), in addition to everything he'd packed earlier in the day, it was uncomfortably heavy.

"So," Jacob said, "you're leaving in, what, two weeks?"

"Thirteen days. But who's counting?"

"Are you ready?"

Ichiro laughed. "No, not even close. I haven't even started to pack yet."

"I meant, are you ready *mentally* to move?"

"Oh." Ichiro thought about the question for a moment. "I guess. It's happening whether I'm ready or not, right?"

Jacob nodded. He detected some doubt in his friend's tone. "It's going to be an incredible experience. I mean, Japan? Seriously? What a cool place to live. You're going to have a blast."

"It does look pretty awesome. I borrowed this travel DVD from the library. Japan is, like, super high-tech. Did you know most video games are released there months before they're available in the rest of the world?"

"You've become quite the library junky," Jacob said.

"And it's all your fault." Ichiro smiled with a mixture of sadness and joy. "Thank you, Jake."

"For what?"

"Being such a great friend. I'm going to miss you."

"I'm going to miss you too."

A few minutes later, Hayden and Hannah coasted down the hill on their bikes.

"Hey, losers," Hannah shouted good-naturedly. "We got our clothes so we're all set."

"And a couple of heavy-duty flashlights," Hayden said.

"Shoot," Jacob said. "I knew I forgot something. Do you have a spare flashlight at home, Ichiro?"

He shook his head. "I only have one. Do you want to go home to get your flashlight and meet us at my place?"

Jacob looked up at the greying sky. He didn't want to

add any more time to their trip. "Nah, forget it. As long as we don't separate I'll be fine."

It started to rain, a light mist that coated their skin.

Hannah clapped her hands. "All right. Let's buy some snacks. Don't forget to get something from each of the four major junk food groups: candy, chocolate, chips and pop."

They argued, debated and made random declarations as they walked into the convenience store and paced its aisles under the watchful eye of The Willow.

"What about Cheezies? What food group do they belong to?"

"They fall under 'chips.'"

"Cotton candy?"

"'Candy,' you fool. It's right there in the name."

"Okay, here's a tough one: chocolate-covered gummies. 'Candy' or 'chocolate'?"

"Neither, because they're disgusting. If anyone buys any chocolate gummies our friendship is over, do you hear me? Over!"

The sound of their laughter was loud and heartfelt. With a box of Nerds in one hand and a bag of Atomic Warheads in the other, Jacob didn't think he had ever felt happier than at that precise moment.

The Willow slapped his hand on the front counter

three times. "Keep it down, you punks. I'm trying to run a respectable business here."

The four friends laughed even louder.

FIFTEEN

Sepequoi Lake was angry. Its water slapped against the canoe and rocked it from side to side. Splashes of foam-white water reached over the gunwales like many-fingered hands and filled the bottom of the boat, soaking their feet. The rain — no longer a gentle mist — drenched the rest of their bodies.

Paddling was a struggle. For every two metres they moved forward it felt like the waves pushed them one metre back.

"Should we turn around?" Hayden yelled over the sound of distant thunder.

This was not how Jacob had pictured the start of their overnighter. He was freezing, his back ached and they had nearly capsized three times, but there was no turning around now, at least not for him. *I can't go back. I have to see this through to the end.*

The beginning of the trip had already been delayed. Twice. First, when they exited East Road Convenience Hayden spotted his father — he was drinking with a couple of buddies on The Wet Whistle's patio. The kids ducked back into the store and watched through the dirty window, hoping he'd leave the bar before long.

The Willow shouted at them nearly the entire time, so Hannah had to buy an extra chocolate bar to placate the old man. They had to wait a while before the twins' father went inside, and then they made their break.

The second setback was the storm that had soaked them to the bone. It held off as they biked to Ichiro's house, but shortly after they got there the rain came down in sheets. They decided to wait longer still as Jacob chewed his nails and watched the sky. When the rain didn't slow down, he convinced the others to leave then and hope for the best.

They did not get the best. Far from it. What they got was the threat of pneumonia and a canoe filled with water.

"We're almost there." Ichiro pointed over the canoe's starboard side. "Look."

Ahead, through the rain that now seemed to be hitting them from all directions, was the faint outline of the island.

They stopped paddling for a moment and stared at the island in silence.

"If anyone is having second thoughts," Jacob said, "you can drop me off, return home and pick me up in the morning."

"We've been over this," Hannah said. "You're crazy if you think we'd leave you here alone overnight."

Jacob nodded and looked back to the island. He had given his friends plenty of outs and they were still with him. The top of the roof and the red-brick chimney peeked out from between the scraggly pine trees that surrounded Summer's End. The wind flung a sheet of rain into his face, and he had to wipe his eyes before he could see clearly again.

"The storm's pushing us too far back," Ichiro said. "Let's keep going before we get any wetter."

Not possible, Jacob thought.

They worked together and slowly neared the island. It was hard work but at least it kept them warm.

Finally, they reached the island.

———

After tying the canoe to the dock post, they trudged through the overgrowth toward Summer's End. The rainwater had turned the path into a creek that flowed down into the lake to join the tumult of crashing waves and churning whitecaps. Jacob slipped in the mud more than once, and his shoulders ached under the strain of the gear on his back.

As they neared the house on the other side of the island, the pungent aroma of churned earth shifted to an acrid smell, something bitter like swamp gas and rot.

They broke into the clearing and came face to face

with Summer's End once more.

Ichiro slipped the tent bag off his back and opened its drawstring. "This isn't going to set itself up, so let's get to work."

"The tent?" Hannah said, incredulous. "Why not go straight inside?" She gestured at the house.

The three boys looked at Hannah in shock.

"Spend the entire night in there, with the doctor and all the other ghosts?" Hayden said. "You can't be serious."

"I can be, and I am."

"We'll go in soon," Jacob said. "But it's not a bad idea to have a home base out here. Somewhere to keep our stuff, somewhere to meet up if we get separated."

Hayden and Ichiro both nodded in agreement.

"Fine." Hannah swiped the tent bag out of Ichiro's hands and began pulling out the poles. "Babies."

They set about assembling the tent, trying to keep the inside dry, a losing battle. Jacob opened a small nylon bag and pulled out the metal pegs to ground the tent.

"Do you have a hammer?" he asked Ichiro.

"Isn't there one in the bag?"

They all stopped what they were doing and searched for the hammer, but it didn't turn up.

"It must have fallen out somewhere," Ichiro said.

"Not a problem," Jacob said. He picked up a large rock and crouched in front of the first peg. He raised it in the air but paused. The rock nearly slipped out of his fingers.

"What's wrong?" Ichiro asked.

"Nothing," Jacob said. But it wasn't nothing. For a brief moment the tent peg had looked like a cardinal. He shook his head and hammered the peg deep into the ground before it could change shape again.

———

They sat in a wet tent in wet clothes, watching the grey light fade as the sun set somewhere in the distance behind the clouds.

"I'm just going to say it," Hayden said. "This sucks."

No one answered.

Lightning flashed, followed a few seconds later by thunder that shook the ground beneath them.

"That was close," Hannah said. "It might've hit the island."

"If it hit the island," Hayden said, "there wouldn't have been a pause between the lightning and the thunder. We would've seen and heard them at nearly the same time. It more likely hit the mainland."

"Thanks, Encyclopedia Brown."

Hayden rolled his eyes.

The sides of the tent whipped and cracked like a flag in a tornado as the wind howled through the trees. If they hadn't been sitting inside the tent and weighing it down, Jacob wondered if the pegs would be enough to hold the tent in place.

Another flash of lightning electrified the sky, followed a second later by thunder so loud it popped Jacob's ears. There was a splitting crack, the sound of something big falling, a crash of wood colliding with wood and a mighty splash.

"What was that?" Hayden asked, removing his hands from his ears.

Ichiro worked it out first. "It sounded like a tree falling on something." His mouth fell open. "The dock." And then, "*Scarlet Sails!*"

Hannah unzipped the tent and jumped outside. The others followed, squinting their eyes and shielding their heads with their jackets. They ran single file down the path toward the island's shore, slipping and sliding in the mud. Hannah stopped at the water's edge. The three boys bumped into her back, one after the other.

A tree had fallen, just as Ichiro had guessed. A bolt of lightning had struck it near its base and cracked it in half. It had toppled onto the dock, crushing the rickety structure beneath its weight. One half of the dock was pinned between the tree and the shoreline. The other half was gone.

Hayden spoke first. "Where's the canoe?"

Jacob scanned the lake but saw nothing floating on the waves.

Lightning streaked down in a jagged vein and struck the mainland, followed shortly by a loud crack and a lingering rumble. As the sound faded they turned and ran back up the hill. There was nothing they could do to get the canoe back. Either it would wash up on shore or it wouldn't. There was a good chance it had been shattered, like the dock. Standing around in the rain wouldn't fix anything, but with a little luck the storm would soon move on. Maybe in an hour or two, if the rain had stopped, they could split up, take their flashlights and search the shore around the island for the canoe.

They ran into the clearing and stopped dead in their tracks as more bad luck befell them.

A swooshing gust of wind streaked across the ground and entered the tent through its open flap, picking it up in the air as easily as a paper bag. Hannah jumped and caught one of the tent pegs, but it was covered in mud and slipped through her fingers. They watched helplessly as the tent rose into the air and became entangled in the upper branches of a pine tree. The needles tore and ripped and clawed at the tent, slashing the nylon siding like a starved predator falling upon its captured prey.

"C'mon," Hannah said, as they picked up their belongings. "Let's go inside!"

"No way," Hayden said. "We already took a vote, remember? We're not spending the whole night in there."

Hannah pointed at the ruined tent, impaled by the tree and thrashing in the wind. "You want to climb up there and make your bed, be my guest. Me, I'm going inside." She turned and ran through the rain to the house without waiting for a reply.

Ichiro followed. Jacob looked at Hayden and shrugged. "It's not ideal, but she's got a point."

Hayden shook his head. He couldn't make eye contact with Jacob. "I've got a bad feeling in my gut, like I'm going to be sick."

Jacob watched Hannah and Ichiro step inside and started to feel a little sick to his stomach too. "Let's just go into the front hall and come up with a plan. Maybe the rain will stop soon and we can find somewhere outside to hole up for the night. Whatever we do, we'll stick together. Okay?"

"The front hall. Where the doctor killed his wife and himself."

"We're out of options."

Hayden thought for a moment and then nodded. They walked to the front porch and, after a hesitant moment, walked through the open door. Jacob shut it quietly behind him, sealing them inside.

The front hall was empty. Hannah and Ichiro were gone.

"Hello?" Hayden said, half whispering, half calling.

Silent pause.

"Hannah? Where are you?"

More silence.

"If you're just messing around I'm going to kill you."

Hannah's strained voice came from the shadows: "*Too . . . late . . .*" A split second later, her skull, stripped of skin and flesh, came bounding down the hall toward the front door. It stopped at Jacob and Hayden's feet.

The boys jumped, yelled and turned to run back outside.

Hannah laughed and stepped out of the office. "The look on your faces was priceless."

"Not cool, Hannah," Hayden snapped. "You have no idea how not cool that was."

Ichiro followed Hannah into the hall.

"You were in on this too?" Jacob asked him.

"No," Ichiro said, "but you have to admit, it was pretty funny."

Jacob pushed the skull away with the toe of his shoe. It bounced a few times and came to a stop under the front-hall table. "You seriously thought it was funny that she scared us like that?"

"No, not that," Ichiro said. He held up a square piece of paper. "I found this on the table beside the skeleton. 'Adam Brothers, Real Human Skeleton, Certificate of Authenticity, 1899, Calcutta.' Hannah handled an actual human skull. *That's* funny." He turned to face Hannah. "I hope you didn't, like, put your fingers up inside it."

Hannah's smile faltered. "Quit messing around. It's probably made of plaster or something."

Jacob picked up the smile Hannah had dropped, then took the certificate from Ichiro and confirmed it was genuine. "Nope. That skeleton is one hundred per cent authentic. The real deal."

"Oh, God." Hannah gagged and frantically wiped her hand on her pants. "I stuck my fingers and thumb through the eye sockets and nasal cavity like it was a bowling ball."

"*Shh!*" Ichiro said, silencing them all. "We're not alone." He pointed down the front hall.

At the far end was the shadow of a large man standing perfectly still.

Hannah forgot about the skull she'd just bowled

down the hallway and crept forward, one slow step at a time.

"Hannah, what are you doing?" Hayden hissed.

She waved him off, indicating for him to be quiet, and continued approaching the shadow man.

Jacob hadn't planned on facing the doctor so soon and he felt woefully unprepared. He reached into his shirt and held his mother's necklace, remembering that he didn't even know if the gemstone was chalcedony or not. And even if it was, what good would it do against a surgical knife?

Hannah neared the end of the hall. Dr. Stockwell still hadn't moved. Jacob couldn't believe her courage. He felt he should do something, anything, to help her. What had possessed her to do something so rash, so foolish? She'd never been one to wait for a safety net, but this seemed especially bold, even by her standards.

And then she stopped and laughed. The sound echoed across the hall. She gripped a piece of bubbled, frayed wallpaper near the ceiling and tore a piece off the wall. "It's just a dark water stain." She laughed a little more.

For a moment, just a brief flicker of time that came and went so quickly that it almost didn't seem real, someone in the walls joined in her laughter.

Hannah dropped the strip of wallpaper to the floor and quickly rejoined her friends. "Was that one of you?"

The three boys shook their heads.

"Maybe it was just the walls creaking," Hannah said, but she didn't sound convinced.

Jacob couldn't believe he'd been tricked into believing the water stain had been a man's shadow. He wanted to take a closer look and regretted, again, that he had forgotten his flashlight at home. Then he had an idea. He turned on his phone to use the built-in flashlight, but before he opened the app he noticed that he didn't have a signal.

"What's with this place?" he said to himself. "Does anyone else have a signal?"

Hannah and Hayden turned on their own phones.

"Nothing."

"Not a single bar."

"Ichiro?" Jacob asked.

"No technology for a week, remember?"

"That's just great," Jacob said.

———

Hayden peered out the front window. His eyes held a faraway look. "I could make it, if I needed to. I could swim to shore."

"Not in this storm, you couldn't," Hannah said. "And not in the dark."

"I could. It's not that far."

"No way, Hayden," Jacob said. "It's too dangerous."

"So what now? You won't let me swim for help, we can't call anyone and we have no canoe. And in case you've all forgotten, no one knows we're here."

Hayden was right. They'd told their parents they were sleeping at each other's houses. Their absence wouldn't raise any alarm bells until the morning, maybe later. But that would only be a problem if something went wrong. "Nothing has changed. The plan is the same."

"Right. The plan. I forgot," Hayden said. "We have to somehow trick the doctor into entering a hole in the basement's wall, and then somehow seal the hole up with him on the other side. And everything will then be okay. Somehow."

"I know it's not the world's greatest plan, but it's all I've got."

"Jake is the smartest guy I know," Ichiro said. He pulled his flashlight out of his backpack and turned it on. "If he thinks it will work, then it's our best option. And if he hasn't figured it all out yet, he will."

Ichiro's show of support gave Jacob a much needed, albeit small, boost of confidence. "If anyone else has any other ideas," he said, "I'm all ears."

No one said anything.

"Well, then," Ichiro said. "There's no time like the present. Let's go find this so-called Black Sea."

"This is a bad idea," Hayden said.

"I never said otherwise," Jacob said. "But isn't that why we're here?"

Hayden only shrugged. He and his sister grabbed their flashlights out of their bags. They started down the hall but Hannah stopped them with an outstretched hand. She pointed at the strip of wallpaper that she had peeled off and dropped to the floor.

"It's back up on the wall," Hannah said in disbelief. She peered closer, nearly pressing her face right up against the wall, searching for a tear in the paper but finding none. "You saw me rip it off, right?"

The boys nodded.

She ran her fingers over the wallpaper but couldn't find any torn edges. "So who put it back up, huh?"

"Calm down, sis."

"Don't tell me to calm down. This isn't funny, okay?"

"But the skull, that was funny?" Hayden said. "Look, we've been together the entire time. How could it have been one of us?"

"Then how can you explain it?"

"I can't." Hayden shook his head. "I can't."

The house grew unnaturally silent. Even the storm seemed distant and muted. And as the silence descended upon them, so did a chill that made Jacob's skin crawl.

"Guys," Ichiro whispered urgently. He pointed a trembling finger at something behind Jacob.

Fear swelled in Jacob's gut like an ice-cold ball. He turned slowly as if in a dream, a dream in which he had surrendered control. He wasn't sure he wanted to see what Ichiro was pointing at but he was powerless to look away.

This time, it wasn't a shadow, and it certainly wasn't a water stain. Standing between them and the front door was Dr. Stockwell. Tall and muscular with narrow eyes. They were like scalpels, those eyes, sharp enough to pierce straight through flesh and bone. He was dressed in the same suit and apron he had worn the day Jacob had seen him from the woods. He lifted his surgical case in front of his chest.

"I told you—" He opened the first latch. *Click.* "Not to—" He opened the second latch. *Click.* "Come back here."

He slowly pulled out a surgical knife. It was bigger, sharper, altogether more *real* than Jacob had envisioned in his nightmares.

Dr. Stockwell took a step toward them, then another.

The sound of his boots clomping on the floor sent shivers up Jacob's spine.

His mind raced in a million different directions, envisioning a multitude of horrific outcomes. He managed to quiet his thoughts and yell, "Run!"

In the panic-fuelled chaos that followed, Jacob didn't see where his friends scattered. He ran backwards, unwilling to turn his back on the doctor, but his heel caught on something. He tripped and fell. His back was the first thing to slam into the ground, followed by his head. Jacob's vision spun. Light exploded in his eyes. Despite his pain he sat up quickly.

Dr. Stockwell towered over him, impossibly tall. "Look out," he taunted. His voice was guttural and rough, like chains being dragged over gravel. He raised the knife in the air, preparing to swing it at Jacob.

Jacob leapt to his feet and turned to escape.

Then he saw her. A mere metre down the hall, between him and the stairs, was Tresa. She stood with her hands out, silently staring at Jacob with terror in her wide eyes. Her skin was thin and pale as morning frost.

Go, Jacob commanded himself, *don't stop, just run,* and he did — straight through Tresa's frail body as if she was nothing more than a cloud of mist.

He sped through the kitchen and into the dining

room, slamming the door closed behind him. But if he kept running, he'd enter the parlour with the phonograph and then be back in the front hall.

I'm trapped, he realized.

SIXTEEN

August 27

Jacob stumbled through the dark dining room without thinking to turn on his cellphone's flashlight. He banged his knee on the table. He crouched and peered underneath it, desperate for a place to conceal himself while he collected his thoughts. But he'd be painfully visible under the table.

There's nowhere to hide, he realized. This wasn't a childhood game of hide-and-seek. How was he supposed to hide from Dr. Stockwell? Even if the ghost couldn't see him under the table, Jacob feared he'd be able to hear his heart as it tried to pound its way through his chest: *boom, boom, boom.*

Get a grip, he told himself. *You can't hide, and you can't stay here.*

Think. Think, think, think.

The basement. As little as he wanted to go down into the basement at that particular moment, he knew that's where he had to go.

The door to the parlour was open, a small blessing since he wouldn't have to slow down to open it. If Dr. Stockwell was following him, he'd be coming through the kitchen any moment.

Jacob took a few deep breaths, steeling his nerve. He gripped the side of the table and listened.

Silence.

Ignoring the pain in his knee, he sprinted to the open door.

Except, when he was just a few steps away from it, it slammed shut with a bang that shook the walls. He reached his hands out in front of his face and braced himself as he ran into the door with a grunt.

He didn't know what had happened. He'd been running, the door had been open, and then it wasn't. He'd collided with it and was too dazed and shocked to think of an explanation.

But then he heard her.

Right behind him.

"Hello, young man," said a woman's voice, a voice he had never heard before. But he knew instantly who it was. "I've been expecting you."

Jacob turned and pressed his back against the door. He could see very little in the dim light, only the faintest outline of the table, the chairs and a person sitting at the opposite end of the room.

"Don't be frightened. I'm not going to bite you. Turn on a light and see." Tresa spoke with a slight German accent and her words hung in the air like a waft of smoke.

Jacob didn't want to oblige Tresa, but felt he had to nonetheless. He reached into his pocket, pulled out his phone and noticed that it was after three thirty. He turned on the flashlight. The light twitched across the walls thanks to his shaking fingers. It settled hesitantly on Tresa, seated at the head of the table. She smiled.

"See? I'm not so bad, am I?"

"You're not real," he said.

"Come, now," Tresa said. "You're talking to me. That makes me real. Why don't you sit?"

"That's not what I meant. You're not really *alive*." He kept the quivering light trained on her face while he moved his other hand blindly behind his back in search of the doorknob. "You're Tresa, aren't you?" Perhaps if he distracted her she wouldn't notice that he was trying to escape.

"What a clever boy you are." She clasped her hands and nodded. "But not clever enough by half. You'll find that door quite locked."

His fingers finally found the knob. It didn't turn when he tried to twist it.

"See? I always tell the truth."

How could the door be locked? It had just closed a moment ago. Jacob tried to turn the knob more forcefully, no longer caring if Tresa saw him trying to escape, but it didn't budge. He looked at Tresa and his

226

eyes settled on the door to the kitchen behind her.

"Also locked," Tresa said.

"What are you doing?" Jacob said, his confusion being replaced by panic. "I came to save you, and the children. I knew Colton. I think I can stop your husband once and for all."

"Please rest assured that I'm not trying to lock you in, Jacob. I'm trying to lock *him* out. I can stop him, but not for long. It's safer in the basement. He hates the basement."

"How do you know my name?" Jacob felt on the verge of tears. Nothing made sense. His world had flipped upside down.

"I know everything that happens in my house. Everything." Her smile disappeared for a moment, but Tresa was quick to summon it back. She even managed to laugh demurely. "Please, sit."

"No."

"I insist."

The chair opposite Tresa slid away from the table, its clawed feet scraping over the floorboards. Reluctantly he sat, but he kept his back straight and his legs tensed, ready to spring back to his feet if need be. But where would he go? With a sickening feeling in his gut it dawned on him that he was totally at Tresa's whim.

Why was she slowing him down? *She's crazy*, Jacob

thought. *Completely insane.* How could he blame her after everything she had been through, first in life, then in death?

While trying to devise an escape plan, Jacob figured he might as well keep her talking. "I know what he did. I know he killed you and a couple of children and himself. I think he's somehow managed to keep on killing kids over the years."

"Is that what you think?"

Jacob swallowed and nodded. "I read about it in the newspaper. He used one of his surgical knives."

Tresa sighed and turned her gaze downwards, then nodded. "You can't imagine what it feels like to have your belly sliced open, to have your intestines spill out through your fingers." She cupped her stomach gently as if her cut had reopened. "Death didn't come for me immediately. I was alive for a few minutes, lying beside my husband while I watched our blood pool around us in the hall. It felt like an eternity." She buried her face in her palm. "Sometimes it feels like I didn't die at all. I get so confused."

Jacob let her words wash over him without stopping to allow them to fully sink in. If he thought about what was happening, this conversation with a confused, sorrowful dead woman, he was afraid he might start to break down himself. "He was upset that you couldn't have children, wasn't he? Is that why he killed the first couple of kids?"

"Have you ever seen someone die from tuberculosis?"

Jacob shook his head, realizing Tresa wouldn't know that TB was no longer an epidemic.

"It's a dreadful sight to behold. They called it the Great White Plague in Europe. It destroys the lungs, causing fever, weight loss and coughing of blood. My husband didn't kill the first two children. They died on their own." Tresa's glassy eyes had a faraway look. "But they didn't stay dead, did they? No, they did not." Then, as if she'd just realized she had said something she shouldn't have, her eyes snapped back into focus and she covered her mouth with her hand.

Her shock emboldened Jacob, if only a little. "Their souls remained."

Tresa sat in silent contemplation for a long time. Just when Jacob thought she might not say another word, she spoke.

"This island is special," she said. "It kept those children here, as if it knew they were too young to die. Sharon Kennedy and Jeremy Langdon. And just like that, James and I had the children we always wanted."

Jacob had a hard time concealing the thought that popped into his head: *They weren't yours to keep.*

Tresa continued. "A third child, Patty Anderson, died

shortly after Sharon and Jeremy, but not from TB. She died in a house fire after she left the island, her TB cured. My husband stayed up late, waiting for her to return, but she didn't. It became apparent that in order to remain here forever, the children had to die here. When James realized that, he . . . he . . ."

Jacob didn't finish her sentence for her, fearful she'd get angry and stop talking. But any fear he had felt when she had first appeared in the dining room was slowly turning into pity. Tresa was weak and damaged, both of body and mind.

"He killed him — an innocent boy, Danny Fielding. His health was improving. He was only six." She buried her face in her hands and sat quite still. If she was crying, she was doing so without a sound. Jacob seized the opportunity to scan the room, still looking for a way out. He saw nothing new: two locked doors, one table, twelve chairs and one hutch.

But in that hutch was cutlery. If he could somehow retrieve a knife and use it to pry open the door's lock, he might be able to break free. The locks were old. Hopefully they'd be weak with age.

"Am I boring you?" Tresa asked, looking up.

Jacob whipped his head back to her. "I'm sorry. My eyes drifted, that's all. What happened to Danny after he died?"

She stared at him for a while before responding. "He stayed with Sharon and Jeremy, proving that anyone who dies here stays here. When I found out what my husband had done, I was sickened. I couldn't sleep, couldn't eat. I was terrified of James, of the monster he'd become, but I knew I had to do something so I decided to go to the police. He stopped me in the front hall as I was leaving. He no longer trusted me and told me I couldn't leave the island again. I tried to fight past him, and that's when he cut me." She laughed bitterly. "Of all the things that could have gone through my head as I lay dying, my last thought was that I would never have children of my own. My husband then stabbed himself in the heart, and like the children, our souls remained here."

The story fit with what Jacob had expected, but hearing it told first-hand from one of the murder victims made it all the more gruesome, shocking and tragic.

Suddenly, Tresa cocked her head to the side and her eyes went wide. "Did you hear that?"

"No," Jacob said in a panic. "What is it?"

A moment passed that was fraught with anxiety.

Tresa finally said, "It's my husband. He's coming. Get to the basement. I'll stop him for as long as I can."

Jacob jumped to his feet and upended the chair behind him. He heard the parlour door unlock, and it swung open a crack. Without waiting to see what Tresa planned on doing when Dr. Stockwell arrived, Jacob dashed out of the dining room, through the parlour, across the hall, into the doctor's office and nursery and into the adjoining room, past the old cots and down the rickety stairs. Blood pumped through his veins and his head began to pound.

As he took the stairs three at a time, Jacob could have sworn Tresa whispered one final warning directly into his ear.

He can never have too many children, and it's time for him to claim one, two, three, four more . . .

But she wasn't there. Had the voice been his imagination? There was no way to be certain.

The final step snapped in two under Jacob's weight, and he pitched forward into the dark, landing with a crash on the dirt floor. His cellphone flew from his hand and skidded away in the shadows. He inhaled a cloud of dirt and coughed violently. The humid air smelled just as bad — no, worse — as the first time he and Ichiro had stood at the top of the stairs and looked down. The reek of death was so strong in the basement that it burned Jacob's nostrils every time he inhaled. He tried breathing through his mouth but it wasn't much better. After a moment, he got to his knees, then to his feet.

Although it was so dark that he couldn't see his hand

in front of his face, he knew with absolute certainty that he was not alone. He felt eyes on his back and a slight breeze on his skin, as if from a passing body. And then he heard a faint whisper.

"Are you alive?" said the child's voice. "Or are you dead?"

SEVENTEEN

"Who said that?" Jacob demanded of the dark. "Who's there?"

The basement could have been large or small, completely barren or filled with unspeakable things — he had no way to tell. The uncertainty — the unknowing — made him feel anxious and claustrophobic.

"Ichiro? Hannah? Hayden?"

No one answered.

Although all he wanted was to dig himself into a deep hole, he knew he couldn't let his fear get the better of him. He couldn't freeze. He had to act.

Jacob got down on his hands and knees and crawled forward slowly. The right side of his body ached where he had landed at the foot of the stairs, but he gritted his teeth and tried not to groan in pain. He swept his hands through the dirt in a wide arc as he inched his way into oblivion. He hoped his searching fingers would land on his phone. He prayed they wouldn't touch anything else.

He heard something scuffle near his hands. It could have been anything: a large insect, a rodent or even a small human.

The cool sensation of metal touched his fingertips as his right hand landed on something in the dirt. He ran his fingers along the object's edge and realized it wasn't his phone. The metal rounded up from the ground. It was a wheel.

He planted his left hand in the dirt to push himself up, and with a stroke of luck, found his phone.

Jacob stood and turned it on. The battery had twenty-two per cent power remaining. He hoped it would be enough to do what he needed to do, and turned on the flashlight.

An old, rusty wheelchair sat empty in the middle of the floor. It rolled backwards ever so slightly, no more than a millimetre, issuing a brief but jarring groan. Had he bumped it when he stood up?

The chair was rather small. Covered in dust, its cracked leather seat had two rounded indents where legs had worn it down, forever leaving their mark.

Jacob turned his back on the wheelchair and slowly scanned the rest of the basement. He hoped to find it filled with normal storage items — boxes, furniture and old clothes — and nothing else. But he found no such reassurance.

Near the back wall was an ornate bookcase filled with ancient medical textbooks, more than a few devoted to tuberculosis and its treatment. In front of the case was a wide wooden table. On its surface, neatly arrayed in precise rows, was a variety of archaic surgical tools: scalpels, drills, saws, scissors, rubber tubes, a blunt metal hammer and rods that resembled railway spikes.

Jacob's eyes wandered over the equipment that had been intended to save lives, and he felt sickened at the knowledge they had been used to take lives instead.

Crackle, crackle, he thought.

It was nearly too much for his mind to handle. He wanted to get out of the basement, fast, but he knew he couldn't. Not yet.

Behind him, the wheelchair's rusty wheels squealed. Jacob spun and pointed his light at it. It was still empty and appeared to be in the same spot as he had last seen it.

Scratch-scratch-scritch.

The sound came from his right. He swung the light to the side but there was nothing there, just an empty corner. But there was something on the wall, scrapes or markings of some kind.

He crossed the basement to examine the wall more closely.

They were letters. Twelve sets of two, crudely etched into the wall by hand and knife.

WC

~~SK~~

SR

BC

~~DF~~

RS

YG

OL

~~JL~~

~~PA~~

HN

ED

Three sets of the initials had been crossed out, while a fourth set had been crossed out twice. It didn't take Jacob long to figure out the grave significance of the letters.

PA must stand for Patty Anderson, the girl who died after she left the island and didn't return. SK and JL are Sharon Kennedy and Jeremy Langdon, the two children who died from tuberculosis and remained. And DF is Danny Fielding, Dr. Stockwell's first murder victim. These must have been the last twelve children who were treated here.

Jacob reached out his hand to trace Danny's crossed-out initials, but his fingers met a subtle but deliberate resistance in the air a centimetre from the rough brick, as if pushed back by a magnetic field. His hand suddenly felt unnaturally cold.

The unpleasant feeling made him flinch. He recoiled, then stubbornly pushed back, determined to touch the wall for no reason other than to prove that he could. Jacob succeeded, but his hand didn't stop at the letters and brick. It passed straight through.

Before he could react — before he knew what had happened — a small hand from within the wall grabbed his wrist with a firm, icy grip.

Jacob yelled as loud as his lungs would allow.

Time slowed down. A chill went up Jacob's arm, making the blood in his veins feel like ice water. He pulled back with as much force as he could, but he wasn't powerful enough to break free of whatever held him from the other side of the wall. He continued to yell. The initials shimmered and floated in circles on the brick surface. At first he thought he was hallucinating or about to pass out, but then he realized that this was the Black Sea Albruna had written about in the journal.

Behind his back he heard feet thunder down the stairs.

"Jake!" Ichiro shouted in panic. "Jake! What's happening?"

Jacob opened his mouth but couldn't speak. It was as

if his throat had been filled with cement and someone had ripped out his tongue.

Hannah joined them, then Hayden. Their flashlight beams danced over the floor and walls.

Ichiro grabbed Jacob's shoulders and pulled him away from the wall. Their combined strength must have caught the attacker off guard, and Jacob managed to yank his hand free of the wall. But a child's hand was clamped on to his wrist like a bear trap. And the child — still concealed by the wall — refused to let go.

"What is that?" Hayden shouted in shock and disgust.

The world around Jacob was growing colder and darker by the second. He didn't know how much longer he could hold on — to his footing, his sanity, his life . . .

"Get it off me!" he pleaded, finally finding his voice. "Get it off me!"

Hannah grabbed the child's fingers and tried to peel them off Jacob's wrist. A shiver jolted through her body like an electrical current, but she managed to hold on.

A second hand reached out through the wall and grabbed Hannah's wrist. She screamed and pulled backwards. Ichiro pulled Jacob's shoulders again. And Jacob used his last shred of strength to dig in his heels and lean back. It was enough to free them, and all three landed beside each other on the ground. It was also enough to pull the child through the wall.

It was Colton. Still ten years old, but up close his pallid skin and sunken eyes made him look like an old man on his death bed. He landed on top of Jacob, Hannah and Ichiro. They yelled again and tried to push Colton away, but their hands passed straight through his small body.

A faint pulse of red light lit Colton's face and the space directly around Jacob. Before Jacob could figure out what had created the light, the air crackled and Colton flew backwards.

Hayden jumped out of Colton's airborne path, while Jacob, Hannah and Ichiro retreated on all fours like a cast of scurrying crabs.

Colton landed in a heap a metre or two away. He jumped up, surprisingly fast and agile for how sickly he appeared. He looked at each of the four friends in rapid succession, as if determining what to do, who to attack first. But when his eyes settled on Jacob, he smiled. "You came back to save me," he said.

Jacob rubbed his wrist. His skin was bruised in the distinct shape of four thin fingers and a thumb. "Yes, I did. Are you . . . are you okay?" Jacob wondered again what had created the bright light that had seemingly sent Colton flying through the air, and then he remembered his mother's necklace. Had it actually worked the way he had hoped, creating the same effect as Albruna's chalcedony necklace? "I didn't mean to hurt you. These are my friends." He motioned to Ichiro, Hannah and Hayden. "Do you remember them? They went — they go," Jacob corrected himself, "to our school. You don't have to be afraid of them."

Hayden, Hannah and Ichiro looked too shocked to speak.

"I remember them," Colton said. He took a few steps forward. Ichiro and the twins all took reflexive steps backwards, but Jacob fought the desire to do the same and stood still. Colton bent to the ground and picked up his red hat, which had fallen when he'd been rocketed off Jacob, and put it back on his head.

"I saw Dr. Stockwell in the hall earlier," Jacob said. He cast a nervous glance at the stairs, fearful that the mere mention of the doctor's name would summon him. "Do you know where he is now? Does he come down here often?"

Colton shook his head. "I don't know where he is, but if she comes down, he'll come down. And she comes down a lot." In a whisper, he added, "They'll both come soon if they hear me talking, if they discover I'm out of the Black Sea."

Jacob's mind raced as he worked out what to do next. "All right, we can use that to our advantage." He pulled the necklace over his head. It glinted green in the flashlights' beams. "This is what propelled you off of us. The stone is chalcedony, and somehow it repels . . ." Jacob stopped himself before he said *ghosts*. He restarted. "If I can push Dr. Stockwell into the Black Sea, then hang this on the wall, maybe using one of those rods on that table as a hook, I don't think he'll be able to get out again."

"Why would you want to stop the doctor?" Colton asked. He looked genuinely confused.

Jacob sighed, realizing the boy knew so little about what had happened to him. He didn't even seem to know he was dead. "Colton," he said gently, "I'm sorry, but . . . Dr. Stockwell killed you four years ago."

"No, he didn't."

"He did. He killed a child back in 1915, and after he killed himself he's killed another kid every four years. It's why so many kids have gone missing over the years. It's why the whole town believes in the Kalapik. Dr. Stockwell is the Kalapik."

"No, he's not," Colton said. He hesitated, but then allowed something he'd been holding back to pass his lips. "Mother is the Kalapik."

After all he'd been through, Jacob almost laughed. Mrs. Cannington hadn't looked good when they'd talked, but she certainly wasn't dead. "Your mom is still alive. She misses you. She asked me to help you. She's definitely not the Kalapik."

Colton's face grew taut and he looked at his feet. "I didn't mean *my* mother. I meant Mother. She makes us call her that. She's evil."

A pit swelled in Jacob's gut, threatening to swallow him whole. He knew — deep down in his very core he knew — but he had to ask it anyway. "Who's evil, Colton? Who makes you call her Mother?"

"Tresa." Colton looked at the staircase as if he was afraid Tresa might stalk down the steps at any moment. "She threatens us. Yells at us. She hates it when we leave the Black Sea. She killed us. All of us."

Jacob took an involuntary step backwards. He felt like he'd been hit by a truck. "No," he said, shaking his head. "No, no. That can't be. The doctor killed all the kids. He killed her too, and himself."

"Is that what she told you?"

Jacob nodded, remembering the conversation in the dining room while simultaneously wishing he could forget it.

"And you trusted her?"

Jacob couldn't speak. He had no words.

"She lied. All her words are lies. She'll say anything, do *anything*, to get what she wants. And all she wants . . ." Colton raised his eyes slowly. "Is a family."

A dead silence fell upon the group as the truth sunk in like a knife to the heart.

Dr. Stockwell wasn't the ghost to be feared.

Mrs. Stockwell was.

Back in the front hall, when the doctor had towered over Jacob and yelled at him to look out, he must've been trying to protect him from Tresa.

Jacob recalled his mother warning him never to swim alone. She had described the Kalapik as a man who lived at the bottom of the lake, stole children who disobeyed their parents and kept them with him forever.

Tresa wasn't a man and she might not live at the bottom of a lake, but everything else lined up all too perfectly, sickeningly so.

She was collecting children. If she couldn't have one in her life, she'd harvest them in her afterlife.

A voice broke the tense silence. It floated down the stairs like water traversing a gentle slope, covering a hint of malice.

"Colton?" Tresa said. "Are those my four new children I hear you talking to down there?"

EIGHTEEN

In the trembling illumination of their flashlights, they saw Tresa's feet first. Her feet alighted briefly on each step without a sound. Her dress — Jacob hadn't noticed it in the dining room, but now he recognized it as the first one Hannah had pulled out of the master bedroom dresser a few weeks ago — swirled around her legs. Her hands came next, long and thin and pale, followed by her chest, her neck and her face. Her mouth was open and her teeth gleamed. Her pale skin glowed faintly in the dark as if she was lit from within. When she reached the bottom of the stairs, her dark eyes regarded Jacob and his friends. Jacob had heard of hungry eyes before, and that's how he thought of hers.

"Oh, good," Tresa said. "You've all met Colton. You're going to be friends. No, more than that. You're going to be siblings."

"We know what you did," Jacob said forcefully, taking a step backwards while trying to buy some time. "You killed your husband, not the other way around."

Tresa held a finger to her thin lips. "*Shh.* You're upsetting your brother."

Colton had backed himself into a corner, where he cowered and shook.

"He's not upset by us," Jacob said. "He's afraid of you."

"Don't be silly," Tresa said. "You're not afraid of me, are you, Colton?"

Colton didn't look at her, but said, "No, Mother."

"You see? I love my children, and they love me. I will protect them with every ounce of my strength, every fibre of my being — just as I will keep you four safe. It's time you met the others." With a nod she indicated the wall and what lay behind it, the Black Sea. "They're dying to meet you."

What happened next surprised Jacob. Hayden — not Hannah — charged at Tresa and threw all his weight into the frail woman. Although she saw the attack coming, Tresa didn't brace for the impact or even step aside. Hayden passed straight through her and landed heavily on the ground. Tresa spun, laughed and grabbed a handful of Hayden's hair.

"You will be first to go through." Tresa dragged Hayden across the floor.

Hannah yelled and ran at Tresa, but Tresa grabbed her around the neck, pinning her where she stood.

"Wait your turn," she hissed, and then tossed Hannah aside like a bored cat disposing of a dead mouse.

"What do we do?" Ichiro asked Jacob.

They were running out of time. Tresa had nearly dragged Hayden straight across the basement. Another few steps and she'd reach the wall. But if Jacob waited for the perfect moment . . .

"Don't do anything," Jacob whispered.

"What? We can't just stand here and let her take Hayden."

"We're not going to let that happen," Jacob said. He held up the necklace but kept the pendant concealed in his palm. "When she gets close enough to the Black Sea—"

"You hit her with that and push her in," Ichiro said, nodding. "It's crazy but it might just work."

I just hope nothing happens to Hayden, Jacob thought.

A moment before Tresa reached the wall, a new voice shouted down from the top of the stairs. "Let him go," Dr. Stockwell said.

Tresa stopped and turned to face her husband. "No, James. He's trying to escape. I'm doing this for his own good. He'll see. He'll come to love me, just like the others."

"He's not yours to take." The doctor walked down the stairs and pointed his knife at Tresa. "He belongs here in this world. Not in there, forever in limbo," he said, moving the knife to point at the Black Sea.

"Don't you dare take another step," Tresa said with malice. "He belongs with me. He belongs to me. They all do."

"No. I've let this go on far too long. This ends to-night." He jabbed his knife at her head but she ducked underneath it. Before Dr. Stockwell could swing again, Tresa grabbed his apron and pulled him off his feet. Although he was much bigger than her, she possessed an inhuman strength.

Maybe he wasn't expecting her to fight back. Maybe, after all the years stuck in Summer's End, he simply had no fire left in his soul. Maybe she had the power of a mother's love and an unbreakable will to protect her children. Whatever the cause — however Tresa managed at that moment to overcome her husband — she spun and flung him at the wall. He passed straight through it and was gone.

Tresa shouted in triumph. "It will take him a long time to find his way back through the wall. He was always so meddlesome, protecting children by scaring them off the island. But there's no one left to protect you now, is there?" She grabbed Hayden and readied to shove him into the Black Sea. "Except for me."

"Why did you kill your husband?" Jacob shouted. It was the first thing that came to his mind, and he hoped it would make Tresa pause. "If it's only children you want, a . . . family, why kill him? And why write a fake letter to your sister making it seem like he was the one who was about to kill you?"

Luckily, it worked. She stopped and turned toward Jacob. The smile that spread across her face was a hideous thing, twisted and revealing too much of her teeth. "The letter was clever, wasn't it? I had hoped someone would find it sooner, but I'm glad you finally did. I took great pleasure thinking the police would discover it and blame my husband for the deaths, but as it turned out, the letter wasn't necessary — the authorities were eager to point their fingers at him without it. Why did I kill James? Well, the night Danny . . . died . . . James found out. About everything. He tried to leave, threatened to go to the police. So I stabbed him in the heart."

"And then you killed yourself."

"Of course. I had to be with my children, my beautiful family. My only regret is that I didn't first claim the eight children who were still alive upstairs." She pointed at the wall and the initials, eight of which were uncrossed. "I look at their initials whenever I need to remind myself of my failure. Never again. So I wait four years between reapings, just the right amount of time so as not to arouse too much suspicion."

His plan had worked. Tresa had relaxed her grip on

Hayden, and the entire time she had talked Jacob had been steeling his nerve. He squeezed the necklace in his hand. It dug into his flesh. This had to work. It had to.

And if not, they were dead anyway, so he had to try.

He lunged forward with all the strength he had. She was shocked, caught off guard and slow to react. Jacob collided with Tresa and pushed her the remaining distance to the wall. Hayden tumbled sideways, free.

Jacob raised the necklace. He shoved the gemstone in her face.

Nothing happened.

Tresa looked from Jacob's face to the pendant and back again. "That's a lovely necklace," she said, in a mocking tone.

Jacob knew Tresa could have overpowered him then, but she seemed content to draw the moment out, to toy with him. "I don't understand," he said quietly, willing the necklace to start working, to send her through the wall. "Colton flew off me when he touched this. Your sister's journal mentioned chalcedony; it's supposed to repel ghosts."

"Oh, it most certainly does. But that," she pointed at the gemstone, "is not chalcedony."

How could he have been so wrong? He'd read Albruna's journal so carefully.

The journal. The journal had only been one half of what he needed to stop Tresa.

The hallway.

Cannington.

A pendant in the shape of the letter C.

In the hallway.

Not in Mrs. Cannington's house.

In Summer's End.

The necklace they had found taped to the back of the photo frame the first day they entered the house.

The necklace Ichiro had dropped when they ran outside.

The necklace Hannah had found under the front-hall table and claimed as her own.

Please let her still be wearing it, Jacob prayed.

"Hannah!" he shouted, making everyone in the basement, even Tresa, flinch. "Throw me your necklace!"

She clued in immediately. She ripped the necklace off her neck and threw it to Jacob in one fluid motion, with all the accuracy of a natural pitcher.

Jacob grabbed it out of the air and pressed it against Tresa in one swift motion. It immediately grew red-hot.

The final sight Jacob had of Tresa — a vision that would haunt him for years to come — was of her mouth agape in shock and her black eyes festering with fear.

The light of the necklace coated her face like a spray of blood.

And then she rocketed backwards and disappeared through the wall.

Jacob laughed — part joy, part hysteria. Ichiro joined in, then Hayden, still a little dazed from being dragged across the floor by his hair. Finally, Hannah laughed as well.

"You did it!" Hannah said, wrapping him up in a tight hug. "You saved my brother! You saved all of us."

"Yeah," Jacob said. His hands were shaking and he felt like he might throw up on his shoes at any moment. "I guess I did." He just hoped Tresa would take as long to find her way back through the wall as she had said her husband would.

Hannah released Jacob and hugged her brother. "Thank you," she said. For once — maybe the first time ever — he had protected her, not the other way around. "That was very brave."

Hayden blushed. "You would've done the same for any of us."

"Hello?" Ichiro said, drawing the word out. "I helped too. Have you all forgotten that I was the first to charge into the basement when Jacob yelled, and tried to pull him free?"

"Of course we haven't forgotten that," Jacob said. He

gave Ichiro a backslapping hug. "Thank you. I promise that if a ghost ever nearly yanks you through some sort of portal into some sort of paranormal dimension, I'll try to pull you free too."

"I'll hold you to that," Ichiro said.

Colton slowly emerged from the shadows where he had remained hidden since Tresa appeared. "I can't believe it," he said with a bewildered look, staring at the place his captor had stood only a moment ago.

Jacob was suddenly painfully aware that Colton was now safe, but that the other children Tresa had killed over the years were still in the Black Sea. And not only were they still in there, but they were still in there with Tresa.

"I'm going to hammer a rod into the wall above the initials and hang the necklace from it so Tresa won't ever be able to come out," he said. "But, Colton, is there any way we can get the other kids out first?"

Colton considered the question for a long time before shaking his head morosely. "No. They don't stray anywhere near the wall. They're too afraid of Mother. I could go in after them . . . but I might never make it back out. Or she could get back out." He looked hopefully at Jacob. "We could stay together, the five of us, here."

Jacob shook his head. "We can't stay, Colton. We need to return to our families." He picked up the hammer and a rod from Dr. Stockwell's table of surgical tools.

"But you can't leave me. Please, don't. You have to protect me from . . . her."

Jacob approached the wall to hammer the rod into the top of it, just below where it met the ceiling, but Hannah stopped him wordlessly and took the tools from his hands. Her meaning was clear: *I'll do the hammering; you talk to Colton.*

"And we did protect you. Once we get this necklace up, you'll be free from her. I wish we could've done the same for the others." He thought he knew the answer, but he asked the question anyway: "Can you leave?"

"I tried once," Colton said. "There's chalcedony in those rocks that surround the island. It threw me back when I got too close." He began to cry quietly. "I can't leave the island. I won't go back in the Black Sea. And I don't want to stay here in this awful house. I just want . . . I just want to move on."

That reminded Jacob of the last thing Mrs. Cannington had said to him before being whisked away in the ambulance. *If you find my son, if his soul is trapped here, promise me you'll help him.*

When he asked her how he could do that, she had tried to tell him about the necklace. Not in her hall, but in the hall at Summer's End.

"I think there's a way," Jacob told Colton, "and I know what we need to do."

I know what I need to do.

He held up the necklace. "If I hold this stone as close to you as I can, I think you'll . . ." *Die?* Jacob thought. *Is that the word? Can someone who is already dead die a second death?* Then he realized that they had already hit the nail on the head. "I think you'll move on."

"How can you be sure?" Colton asked, part doubt, part hope.

"I can't be. We just have to try."

"I'll fly away. It happened before."

With a frown on his face, Ichiro appeared to be trying to work something out. "Sometimes we passed straight through you and the other ghosts, and sometimes you were able to touch us. Can you . . . control that?"

Colton nodded.

"Then we'll hold you, if you'll allow us," Ichiro said. "Right, guys?"

Hannah and Hayden nodded solemnly.

"Okay," Colton said. "Let's try."

Jacob nodded. "Before we do, I have to tell you something. I'm sorry, Colton, for telling you to prove you weren't scared of the Kalapik. I can't tell you how sorry I am for what happened to you."

"It's all right, Jacob. I had pedalled my paddleboat to

this island before, and I would have done it again. It's not your fault."

Jacob dug his nails into his palms and bit the insides of his cheeks. "I'm still sorry. I always will be."

Hannah stood behind Colton, while Ichiro and Hayden took up positions to the boy's sides. All three hesitated before placing their hands on the dead boy's body.

Colton shook with fear. "If this works, I wonder where I'm going?"

"I don't know," Jacob said, "but wherever it is, I hope your—" He was about to say *father*, but Colton didn't know that his father was dead, and Jacob had no desire to be the bearer of such tragic news. "I hope you have family waiting for you."

He raised the chalcedony.

"Are you ready?"

"Yes, I'm ready," Colton said, in choked rush.

Am I? Jacob asked himself.

By way of answering, he swung the stone at Colton. His hand plunged into the boy's chest, right where his heart should have been. Jacob saw his friends squat and dig in their heels to stop from falling over.

A burst of red light flared within Colton's chest. His red hat fell off as he threw his head back and yelled in pain. He thrashed and fought, but Jacob refused to remove his hand. He wanted to — he wanted nothing more at that moment than to run far, far away — but he held on. It was, he knew, the right thing to do.

The red light spread through Colton's body and filled the basement as if the room had been set on fire. The necklace grew uncomfortably hot in Jacob's hand but he didn't let go.

And then, suddenly, Colton stopped struggling, stopped screaming. He looked straight up at the ceiling as if he was staring at something beyond and whispered, "It's beautiful."

His body turned to mist that held his shape for a second before dissipating. There was an odd fractured moment when Jacob was plunging his hand and the necklace into thin air and his friends were holding nothing, but then they looked at each other and their tense bodies relaxed. No one moved for a long, long time.

NINETEEN

"Did it work?" Ichiro asked.

Jacob shook his head. "I have no idea." He walked to the Black Sea, feeling like he had been through a battle, and slipped the necklace's silver chain over the rod Hannah had hammered into the wall. The chalcedony pendant hung down, blocking the first of the initials carved into the wall's surface.

The other three stood and joined him. They regarded the pendant in silence for a while.

Whether or not Colton had moved on after he'd disappeared and whether or not the necklace hanging on the wall would be enough to keep Tresa in the Black Sea, Jacob couldn't say. But it was the best he could do. And he'd never return to the island to double-check. He was done with this place. It was time to move on.

Each of them seemed to realize that there was nothing else to say. Without looking back, Jacob walked up the stairs. His friends followed.

They moved quickly through the house as if they were living in a dream that had begun as a nightmare. Jacob peered into the parlour as he walked through the front hall. His eyes fell heavily upon the old phonograph. He worried it might start playing its siren song again and wondered if he should destroy it. But he doubted Tresa would be able to control it — or anything else — from the Black Sea. Plus, he didn't want to spend a second longer in the house than necessary. Mostly, he just wanted to go home and see his mom.

With a great sense of relief, they stepped outside and saw that the storm had passed. Light rain misted their faces, but that was passing too. The dark cloud that lingered over the island was blowing away. To the east, an early morning sunrise was breaking across the horizon, golden, bright and warm.

As they walked along the path, insects chirped and buzzed and flitted through the cool air.

"I'm sorry," Jacob said. "I put you all in danger by bringing you here, trying to make things right with Colton."

"I believe I speak for all of us when I say you couldn't have kept us away," Ichiro said.

"Absolutely," Hannah agreed.

"Actually, I was opposed to coming from the start," Hayden said. He smiled, then laughed.

"I wanted one final summer together that we'd never forget," Jacob continued.

"I think you got what you wanted," Ichiro said.

"You can say that again," Hayden said.

"I think you got what you wanted," Ichiro repeated.

The heat of the sun mingled with a cool wisp of wind that hinted of autumn's approach. The sunlight warmed Jacob's skin and lifted his spirits.

"Woo-hoo!" Hannah shouted. "I just found an Aero bar in my back pocket. It's completely squished and totally melted, but it's still chocolate." She opened the wrapper and passed it to Hayden, then Ichiro. They scooped some out and licked their fingers clean.

"So good," they said in unison.

Jacob savoured the moment and enjoyed watching his friends joke around, even after what they'd been through. *Especially* after what they'd been through.

He'd entered summer dreading the breakup that was destined to come at its close, but now that it was here he found he had made peace with it. *Things will be different, but that's okay. That's life.*

They reached the shoreline. Their canoe was nowhere to be seen. Jacob wasn't surprised. "I guess we either wait for a boat to pass or swim."

"I'm not waiting," Hannah said.

"Me neither," Ichiro agreed.

"Oh, sure," Hayden said. "I suggested swimming last night and everyone looked at me like I was nuts . . ."

Jacob removed his shoes and shirt, then stepped into

the water. He walked a little farther and dived under, then set his mind on the task ahead. The shore of the mainland was far away, but as long as they didn't panic and focused on one stroke at a time, they would make it.

He knew there was no Kalapik beneath them, waiting to pull them down.

At least, not anymore.

The water felt great. It soothed his tired muscles and washed the dirt and sweat off his skin. It lightened his mind as well, and his head felt clearer than it had all summer.

In that euphoric moment Jacob made a decision.

He would try not to hold on to the past. He would cherish every moment with his family and his friends. He would live freely. All his regrets, his fears, his anxieties . . . They had all come to an end.

ACKNOWLEDGMENTS

Writing and editing this book — with all its twists and turns and horrible deaths to keep track of — was hard and exhausting, and I loved every second of the process. It would have been far more challening without the tireless, good-humoured and insightful guidance of my editor, Tamara Sztainbok. I can't thank her enough for all that she has done to make this book a reality.

Writing for Scholastic Canada is like being part of a large, warm and welcoming family, and I'm so happy to have been adopted into it. I have nothing but respect and gratitude for everyone who works there, particularly Andrea Casault for designing the breathtakingly creepy cover for *Summer's End*, copy editor Erin Haggett for her eagle eyes and Diane Kerner, who not only published my first children's book nearly seven years ago, but also suggested I write a young adult novel after I wrote a few volumes of *Haunted Canada*.

Writing wouldn't be possible without the love and support of my real family, all of whom are incredibly understanding when I retreat into my writing cave for hours at a time to stare off into space. (Side note: I *wish* I had a cave. I'm more of a writing nomad, writing wherever I can find a chair and a table or just a chair and my lap or just a tree to lean against or . . . you get the idea.) My wife and kids, in particular, have all the patience in the world and I couldn't love and appreciate them more than I do.

And finally, my readers rock. What good would a book be without someone to read it? I hope you enjoyed reading this little slice of madness as much as I enjoyed writing it. Don't worry, it won't be my last book. It won't be the end.

ABOUT THE AUTHOR

Joel A. Sutherland is the author of *Be a Writing Superstar*, numerous volumes of the Haunted Canada series (which have received the Silver Birch Award and the Hackmatack Award) and *Frozen Blood*, a horror novel that was nominated for the Bram Stoker Award. His short fiction has appeared in many anthologies and magazines, including *Blood Lite II & III* and *Cemetery Dance* magazine, alongside the likes of Stephen King and Neil Gaiman. He has been a juror for the John Spray Mystery Award and the Monica Hughes Award for Science Fiction and Fantasy.

He is a Children's & Youth Services Librarian and appeared as "The Barbarian Librarian" on the Canadian edition of the hit television show *Wipeout*, making it all the way to the third round and proving that librarians can be just as tough and crazy as anyone else.

Joel lives with his family in southeastern Ontario, where he is always on the lookout for ghosts.

Read true stories of Canadian hauntings

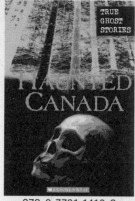

978-0-7791-1410-8

978-0-439-96122-6

978-0-439-93777-1

978-1-4431-2893-3

978-1-4431-3929-8

978-1-4431-4878-8